Cool, competent Margaret Danner didn't need anything from anyone.

Kyle could never reach out to someone like Margaret Danner, but Maggie...Maggie was a different story. He could reach out to Maggie.... He could hold her and comfort her, and he could wipe away her tears. But the most important thing he'd discovered was that he could give her hope.

He didn't want to think about his growing desire to shield and protect her. He didn't know what the chances were of him successfully digging them out. The job was cold, strenuous and painstakingly slow. But the look of promise and hope in Maggie's soft brown eyes was worth any hardship, and made him willing to die trying....

Dear Reader,

At Silhouette Romance we're celebrating the start of 1994 with a wonderful lineup of exciting love stories. Get set for a year filled with terrific books by the authors you love best, and brand-new names you'll be delighted to discover.

Those FABULOUS FATHERS continue, with Linc Rider in Kristin Morgan's *Rebel Dad*. Linc was a mysterious drifter who entered the lives of widowed Jillian Fontenot and her adopted son. Little did Jillian know he was a father in search of a child—*her* child.

Pepper Adams is back with *Lady Willpower*. In this charming battle of wills, Mayor Joe Morgan meets his match when Rachel Fox comes to his town and changes it—and Joe!

It's a story of love lost and found in Marie Ferrarella's *Aunt Connie's Wedding*. Carole Anne Wellsley was home for her aunt's wedding, and Dr. Jefferson Drumm wasn't letting her get away again!

And don't miss Rebecca Daniels's *Loving the Enemy*. This popular Intimate Moments author brings her special brand of passion to the Silhouette Romance line. Rounding out the month, look for books by Geeta Kingsley and Jude Randal.

We hope that you'll be joining us in the coming months for books by Diana Palmer, Elizabeth August, Suzanne Carey and many more of your favorite authors.

Anne Canadeo
Senior Editor

Please address questions and book requests to:
Reader Service
U.S.: P.O. Box 1325, Buffalo, NY 14269
Canadian: P.O. Box 1050, Niagara Falls, Ont. L2E 7G7

LOVING THE ENEMY
Rebecca Daniels

Silhouette
ROMANCE™
Published by Silhouette Books
America's Publisher of Contemporary Romance

If you purchased this book without a cover you should be aware
that this book is stolen property. It was reported as "unsold and
destroyed" to the publisher, and neither the author nor the
publisher has received any payment for this "stripped book."

TYVMFE!—For Jonathan and Christian Fattarsi

Jonathan: Here's to Thursday lunches, Kafka and
Kierkegaard, and nine holes at Swensen.

Christian: Here's to cuddle nights on the
sofa, Slurpees from the 7-Eleven, and solving
the world's problems.

Thanks, guys, for growing up with me.

Your Mom.

 SILHOUETTE BOOKS

ISBN 0-373-08987-2

LOVING THE ENEMY

Copyright © 1994 by Ann Marie Fattarsi

All rights reserved. Except for use in any review, the reproduction
or utilization of this work in whole or in part in any form by any
electronic, mechanical or other means, now known or hereafter
invented, including xerography, photocopying and recording, or in
any information storage or retrieval system, is forbidden without
the written permission of the editorial office, Silhouette Books,
300 East 42nd Street, New York, NY 10017 U.S.A.

All characters in this book have no existence outside the imagination of
the author and have no relation whatsoever to anyone bearing the same
name or names. They are not even distantly inspired by any individual
known or unknown to the author, and all incidents are pure invention.

This edition published by arrangement with Harlequin Enterprises B.V.

® and TM are trademarks of Harlequin Enterprises B.V., used under
license. Trademarks indicated with ® are registered in the United States
Patent and Trademark Office, the Canadian Trade Marks Office and in
other countries.

Printed in U.S.A.

Books by Rebecca Daniels

Silhouette Romance

Loving the Enemy #987

Silhouette Intimate Moments

L.A. Heat #369
L.A. Midnight #431
Fog City #467

REBECCA DANIELS

will never forget the first time she read a Silhouette novel. "I was at my sister's house, sitting by the pool and trying without much success to get interested in the book I'd brought from home. Everything seemed to distract me—the kids splashing around, the sea gulls squawking, the dog barking. Finally, my sister plucked the book from my hands, told me she was going to give me something I wouldn't be able to put down and handed me my first Silhouette novel. Guess what? She was right! For that lazy afternoon by her pool, I will forever be grateful." That was seven years ago, and Rebecca has been writing romance novels ever since.

Born in the Midwest but raised in Southern California, she now resides in Northern California's San Joaquin Valley with her husband and two sons. She is a life-long poet and song lyricist who enjoys early morning walks, an occasional round of golf, scouring California's Mother Lode region for antiques and traveling.

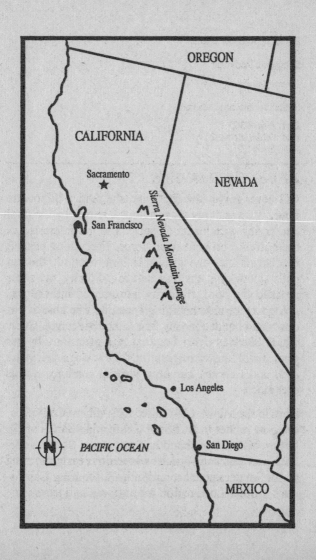

Chapter One

Maggie allowed herself to relax just a little, actually finding that the wind on this cold Sierra morning felt quite pleasant against her face. It was about time, she thought darkly. Her mission on this weekend had been to relax and enjoy herself, but so far she'd done very little of either.

She glared down at the contraption she was sitting on. A snowmobile. What a ridiculous apparatus it was. There was nothing very mobile about it the way it lumbered indelicately through the snow, and it wasn't what you'd call easy to handle. Besides that, it was uncomfortable, exacting and noisy as hell. But she'd been determined to master the thing, one way or another. And after having plodded along the sloping mountain trail above the lodge for almost a half hour now, she thought she finally might be getting the hang of it.

The early-morning air was crisp and had a bite to it, but the sky above was clear and blue. Driving up the mountain last night from Sacramento, through the rugged Donner Pass, she'd heard reports that another winter storm was expected for the Sierras sometime over the weekend, but she couldn't have asked for a more beautiful morning.

However, weather in the area was notorious for changing suddenly and unexpectedly, so she kept a watchful eye on the sky. Of course, being forced inside for the weekend because of bad weather, having to wile away the hours curled up in front of a cozy fire, sipping hot mulled wine and reading a good book, wouldn't exactly upset her, and it would get her off the hook quite nicely. At least she could go back to the office on Monday and tell Jennifer and the others she'd tried her best.

She gazed up at the clear blue sky again and made a face. Just her luck—not so much as a hint of a cloud. It looked as though it was going to be a beautiful day and that left her with no excuse to cancel her cross-country skiing lesson for this afternoon.

Maggie Danner knew her reputation as a workaholic at the prestigious Capitol Mall law offices of Abernathy, Fox and Slone in Sacramento, California, but could she help it if she enjoyed her work? Besides, at thirty-two, she had no husband, no lover, no child and no house—she didn't even have a cat. Her work was her whole life. Lately, though, it seemed as if her entire office staff had taken up the cause to get her away from her desk and convince her to relax more.

Maggie scowled down at the toiling snowmobile beneath her and shook her head again. This was supposed to be relaxing? She found the ungainly thing thoroughly frustrating, but she had to admit she appreciated the concern of her friends—especially her young secretary, Jennifer, who had helped make the arrangements for this weekend. Ever since the young woman had gotten married last year, Jennifer had been on a crusade to marry Maggie off—positive that the lure of hubby, hearth and home was just what she needed in her life. However, as a divorce lawyer, Maggie wasn't as easily convinced.

Still, a weekend away had sounded inviting. Of course, she could have done without running into Kyle Gentry last night after checking in. The man was not exactly a fan of hers. In fact, she probably wouldn't be overstating it to say he hated her. She had been representing his ex-wife, Cindy, in a messy property settlement for over a year now, and things had gotten ugly at times.

Of course, encountering disgruntled mates wasn't anything new for her. In her line of work, acquiring the wrath of her client's "ex" usually just meant she was doing her job well. But finding out she and Mr. Gentry were both guests at the same resort had been a little awkward, and she'd venture a guess that he hadn't been any happier about the discovery than she.

Maggie glanced quickly behind her, surprised to see just how far up the mountain she'd climbed. In the distance below, she could see the smoke curling up from the two large chimneys of the Winter Haven Lodge, creating a quaint, romantic picture. But she

didn't have time to enjoy the picturesque view for
long. The bulky machine below her suddenly jarred
violently, then veered sharply to one side.

Startled, Maggie whirled around and wrested for
control. In her panic, though, she overcorrected the
wheel in the other direction, causing the front skis to
turn and chart a path for a giant redwood directly
ahead. Confused, she threw her weight to one side,
sending the snowmobile swerving sharply. She managed to avoid hitting the tree, but not before getting
smacked across the face by a low-hanging branch.

Snow plummeted from the limbs of the tree, hitting her in the eyes and nose. Blindly she reached for
the brake, cursing to herself. The engine of the snowmobile sputtered and coughed, sending vibrations
through her entire body, but the unwieldy monster finally slid to a stop.

"Oh, don't die, don't die," Maggie murmured,
swatting at the snow in her face. She revved the mo-
tor in the same manner as the attendant at the lodge
had done earlier, working desperately to keep the thing
going. Don't panic, she instructed herself, taking in
huge, deep breaths as she dutifully fueled the temper-
amental engine. She *really* didn't want the engine to
die. She'd only half listened to the instructions the attendant had given her and she wasn't entirely sure she
would know how to get it started again. The last thing
she wanted was to get stuck way up here in the middle
of nowhere and have to climb back down to the lodge
on foot.

Fortunately, though, her panic was short-lived. After a few powerful revolutions, the engine settled down and began to purr quietly.

Maggie sighed in relief. Some relaxation, she thought darkly, reaching up to pull off her knit cap. Her long, shiny brown hair tumbled to her shoulders. She wiped at the snow on her face, but its icy coldness actually felt good against her skin. Despite the frigid temperature, she was burning up inside the insulated leggings and down parka. This snowmobiling just wasn't turning out to be as much fun as everyone had told her it would be. Maybe relaxation just wasn't her thing.

With another resigned sigh, Maggie pulled her cap back on and carefully tucked her long hair into place. There was still the cross-country skiing lesson. Maybe she'd have better luck with that.

She took a deep breath, filling her lungs with the cold, clean air, and timidly started up the trail again. She'd gone only a few feet, when she felt the snowmobile begin to vibrate again. It was just a gentle tremor at first, but the shaking quickly grew more violent.

Now what was the matter with the nasty thing? she wondered as she revved the engine once more. It sounded so noisy, so different. It took her a moment to realize the roar she heard wasn't coming from the snowmobile at all. It came from above her, from up on the mountain.

Had there been some kind of explosion? She listened as the clamoring continued to grow louder and louder. When the vibrations became fiercer, she really became alarmed. Swinging a leg around, she quickly climbed from the snowmobile. The snow-packed ground beneath her feet shook violently. It was an earthquake, she thought, bracing herself against the snowmobile for balance.

But looking up, she realized what was happening had nothing to do with shaky faults and plate tectonics. Roaring like some awful monster unleashed from an icy hell, a wall of white came thundering down the mountain toward her.

Avalanche.

Maggie stood paralyzed, helpless, caught in a haze of horror and fascination. She had to run, she had to take cover, she had to save herself, yet she couldn't seem to move. It was as though her mind had shut down, unable to compute and command. In a panic she turned away, then the violent tremors knocked her to her knees. Somewhere she heard her name being called, but snow and debris were falling too fast for her to see or hear anything else.

She was only vaguely aware of being grabbed from behind, that someone else was there. She was only slightly conscious of being dragged through the tempest, of being pulled into shelter, but nothing seemed real to her at that moment—nothing until she felt herself sandwiched between a cold concrete floor and the weight of a stranger's body.

With reality came fear, and Maggie struggled to fight off hysteria. She couldn't move, could barely breathe, the taste of fear bitter and harsh in her mouth. She felt the need to do something—scream, run, flail her arms and legs about her in unbridled panic. But instinct cautioned her to remain still.

The bedlam outside seemed to go on forever— roaring, ravaging, stealing the sun. Plunged into darkness, the blackness engulfed her. Her fear and confusion were catapulted a degree closer to dread. With the absence of sight, sounds became foremost. They reverberated through her, penetrating every part of her being in a maelstrom of noise and sensation. Pounding, breaking, crashing, banging—those awful noises in the blackness grew louder and more terrifying with each passing moment until she thought she could stand them no longer.

Then...without warning, without preamble... nothing.

It was ironic, she thought as she lay there in the darkness, but the silence felt almost more ominous and more foreboding than the fury had. She hadn't realized she'd been holding her breath until her depleted lungs had her gasping for air. The darkness was so black, and the silence so absolute, she hadn't been sure until that moment that she'd survived the pandemonium.

"Are you all right?"

The voice had been scarcely more than a whisper, but it had shattered the silence almost as violently as the avalanche had shattered the peaceful morning. With the words, perception came rushing back. Suddenly she realized there was a person with her. In the chaos of the avalanche there had been only sensations—confused and fragmented. Now there was a real human being, with warmth, dimension and a voice.

"Hey, can you hear me? Are you all right?" the voice whispered again, giving her a little shake.

Maggie managed to nod, only to realize how fruitless a response that had been in the darkness.

"Fi—" she began, only to have her voice fail. Clearing her throat with what seemed like a scream, she tried again. "I—I'm fine."

She felt him stir and move to one side. Him. Even though the voice had been little more than a hoarse whisper, it had been distinctly male. As he moved away, Maggie was immediately aware of the rush of cold air that displaced the warmth where their bodies had made contact. She heard a small rustling sound; then, in what seemed like a brilliant burst of light, a tiny flame, shattered the darkness.

Maggie stared at the lighter, and then into the face of her rescuer. Suddenly fear rose up again from the depths of her soul. The small flame had brought the horror of her situation to light.

She was alone, in the darkness, with a man who hated her.

Kyle Gentry held the small, disposable lighter up high, trying to cast the light as far as possible. From what he could see, it looked as though the small cabin was still intact, but he couldn't be sure. The only thing he was sure of at that moment was that it had saved their lives. The darkness troubled him, though. The avalanche had buried them—buried them deep enough to block out the sun, and that wasn't a good sign.

He lifted the flame higher, peering uneasily through the darkness to the rafters overhead. The aging beams looked rough and weathered, but sturdy enough. Still, he couldn't help wondering just how much snow it would take to bring the whole roof down on their heads.

"I-is everything all right?"

Lowering the lighter slowly, he looked at the woman beside him and shook his head. This could only happen to him—getting stuck, trapped, with his ex-wife's lawyer. Somebody up there really had it in for him.

"For the moment, anyway," he told her, flicking off the lighter and letting the darkness engulf them again.

Surrounded by the blackness, Maggie felt herself beginning to panic again. "Uh—c-can't you leave that on? I—I mean, it's so dark."

Kyle could hear the fear in her voice and it surprised him. He'd seen her in the courtroom. She was a shark—a lady shark—and he wouldn't have thought she would be afraid of anything. Still, they were a long way from a courthouse. Unfortunately, he had a bad feeling they were a long way from everything.

He flipped the lighter back on and handed it to her. "You hold this while I take a look around," he said, rising carefully to his feet.

"Are we buried very deep?" Maggie asked nervously as she watched him make his way through the darkness to what remained of a rusted, cracked and broken potbellied stove in the corner.

"Hard to say," Kyle mumbled absently, grabbing the stovepipe and giving it a twist. Gesturing with his head, he motioned to her. "Move that light over here a little closer, would you? I want to see if I can dislodge this thing. Careful where you step," he cautioned as she started. "The floor is cracked and uneven."

Maggie stepped gingerly along the rough concrete toward him. "But we can get out, right? I mean somebody from the lodge...you know...a rescue team or something?"

"Oh, sure," Kyle assured her, wishing he could assure himself as easily. "But in the meantime—" The muscles in his broad shoulders strained against his parka as he twisted the rusty pipe. It gave way with a groan, sending soot and snow onto the floor in a gush. Kyle carefully lifted the considerable length of pipe away from the hole and gazed up, hoping he would feel a rush of air, catch a glimpse of light—anything.

There was nothing. Not a breath of air or a trace of daylight. They'd been buried deeper than he thought.

"What do you see?" Maggie asked, watching him expectantly. "Well?" she prompted again when he didn't answer right away. "Do you see anything?"

"Hmm—what? Oh! Uh—no, not—not yet," he mumbled. He glanced over to her. The small flame cast only a dim light, but it was enough for him to see the fear in her eyes. Not to respond to that fear would have been cruel, and Kyle had never intentionally been cruel. He gave her a small smile. "But I've got a few ideas."

For some ridiculous reason, that little smile of his had made her feel enormously better. She felt herself actually smiling back. "Can I help?"

"For the moment, just stand there and hold the light," he told her, picking up the ungainly pipe and fitting it back into its hole in the roof. Once it was in place, he grasped the end of it. "I'm going to—" his voice strained from exertion as he hoisted the pipe upward with a tremendous thrust "—to try and shove this thing up—" He stopped and drew in a deep breath, then strained to pitch the pipe farther upward again. "—far enough to clear the snow and—" he thrust it upward again, casting all of the considerable strength of his upper body to propel the pipe farther still "—bring us in some fresh air."

"Do you really think that's necessary?"

"Necessary?" Kyle repeated, breathless. He stopped and turned to her. Maybe he'd been wrong. Maybe the know-it-all lady lawyer had a better idea.

"Well, I—I mean, they'll be coming soon, won't they?" Maggie stammered, trying her best to not sound panicky. She would prefer that he not know just how frightened she was. "To rescue us, I mean. You said somebody would be coming, didn't you?"

He immediately felt contrite for his caustic reaction. She wasn't being condescending or patronizing. She was scared—maybe even more than he realized.

"Oh, sure, of course," he assured her. "But you know things might be a little crazy there, too. It could take them a while—you know, to organize rescue teams, stuff like that. We might as well do what we can in the meantime, right? No sense taking any chances."

"Of course you're right," Maggie said, feeling foolish. "I'm sorry."

"There's nothing for you to be sorry about," he said quietly. "Now, hold that light up here so I can see."

Maggie watched in silence as Kyle labored tirelessly with the rusted stovepipe. She'd learned a lot about him in the year and half that she'd represented his ex-wife, and yet, until today, she doubted that she'd exchanged more than a half-dozen words with the man. For all practical purposes, they were strangers.

Of course, Cindy Gentry had had plenty to say about her ex-husband—about his temper, his other women, his abuse and his neglect. Cindy had bravely endured the marriage as long as she could for the sake of their son, Conner. But ten years had been enough.

As a professional football quarterback, Kyle Gentry had commanded exorbitant salaries. When a shoulder injury had ended his career prematurely, he'd managed to rally his pro sports career into a successful business. Now, at age thirty-eight, he'd made a fortune in commercial real-estate development and construction in and around California's growing capital city, and Cindy felt she deserved her share. She'd come to Maggie because of her reputation for being tough and for getting her clients what they wanted. And now, nearly two years after the final divorce decree had been filed with the courts, it looked as though that was finally going to happen.

The case that was to decide the property settlement between Kyle and Cindy Gentry had been scheduled to go to trial at the end of this month. Maggie had prepared a strong case, determined to get her client everything she deserved to make up for the years of abuse and mistreatment she'd taken at the hands of this man. One way or another, he was going to pay for the way he'd made his family suffer. But Kyle and his lawyer weren't about to give up anything easily. Maggie had been prepared for a fight, and the trial promised to be long, drawn out and ugly.

That was why it surprised her when Kyle's lawyer, Steven Berg, had called her earlier this week with talk of an out-of-court settlement. Only there had been nothing to "settle" in the arrangement he'd suggested. It seemed that Kyle Gentry was now willing to agree to his wife's demands—all of them, no ifs, ands or buts.

Maggie had to admit she'd been a little surprised by this sudden turn of events. It was highly unusual for an opponent to give you everything you wanted. Of course, as Cindy's lawyer, she couldn't have been more pleased. It was a sweetheart of a deal, and she would have liked nothing more than to take credit for pulling off a stunning victory. But the simple truth of the matter was there had been no hard-fought battle, no well-deserved win—this had been surrender, plain and simple.

Still, who was she to complain? It was a better deal than they ever would have hoped to get from the judge. Cindy had been just as surprised as she at the sudden turn around by her ex-husband, but she'd hardly wanted to question it. Yet Maggie couldn't help but be curious. It had been a very kind, very generous gesture—sparing his family a lot of time and pain. But everything she'd heard about Kyle Gentry told her he wasn't a generous man—or a particularly kind one. What had happened to make him capitulate so completely? Just what type of man was he?

Maggie watched as he worked at a steady pace with the stovepipe. She still didn't know what kind of man he was, but one thing she knew for certain: he was the man who had saved her life. How did she thank him for that? And could she sit across from him at a conference table and watch as he signed his life away?

Kyle rammed the pipe upward, again and again, gradually cutting a path through the snow, inch by careful inch. But each precious gain made the job that much harder. The farther the pipe edged upward, the more awkward the angle it created for Kyle and the more strength it required to continue. But, despite the difficulty of the job, he refused to give up. Even when the rusted edge of the pipe cut through the soft nylon and insulation of his gloves, even when his tired muscles protested and even as the dislodged snow pelted him in the face. But when the pipe rose so high that pushing it became impossible, he finally stopped.

After thinking for a moment, he slipped off his bulky parka. Finding a rickety wood box beside the stove, he turned it onto its side and climbed on top to continue. Finally, after what had to be well over an hour of backbreaking labor, and after he had tunneled almost a full six feet up, a crack of light appeared.

"It's light," Maggie squealed, peering up as cold air rushed down the narrow tunnel. Flicking off the lighter, she tugged on Kyle's pant leg. "You did it. I can't believe it—you did it. You reached the top."

Kyle gave the pipe one last heave upward to lodge it securely in the hole, then climbed down from the wood box. He was exhausted, and his hands fell lifelessly to his side. He looked up the narrow shaft, not knowing whether he should be delirious or despondent. It had taken nearly the entire length of the six-foot pipe to reach the top of the snowbank, indicating, from the peak of the cabin's roof, they were buried beneath nearly six feet of snow. Given the cabin's dimensions, that meant from the ground floor they were almost twenty feet down.

"You'd better sit," Maggie insisted, taking him by the arm and leading him through the darkness. "You look tired."

"I am," he murmured, giving her a little laugh. He looked down into her face as she helped him to the floor, and felt an odd sensation in his chest. Why had it pleased him so to see the fear gone from those dark eyes of hers?

He glanced back over at the narrow tunnel and drew in a deep breath of cold, fresh air. With the flame of the lighter extinguished, the light filtering down the shaft appeared brighter. Though it was scarcely more than a glimmer, it was enough to cut through the inky blackness of the interior of their buried cabin, and for the moment, that was enough.

He turned and glanced at Maggie, who now sat beside him. She wasn't nearly as frightened as she had been in the beginning, and he could understand how she felt. It was a far cry from being rescued, but he had to admit that feeble stream of light made him feel better, too. He'd always thought he'd tried to appreciate life, to make the most of the moment, but catching that small glimpse of sky just now had been like seeing it for the very first time.

But, he thought grimly, they still had a long way to go. Even if the lady lawyer didn't realize it, things still looked pretty bleak for them. Of course, if—and that was a *big* if—by some act of providence or pure luck, the lodge had been spared the devastation, it was reasonable to assume they would be rescued quite soon. After all, they were both guests, and sooner or later their absence would be noted and acted upon.

But Kyle had gotten a good look at the avalanche an instant before taking shelter. It had been enormous, swallowing up everything in its path—and Winter Haven Lodge had been directly in its path. If the avalanche had buried the lodge, it could be days before help arrived, if at all.

He leaned his head back against the rough wooden slat wall. At least they'd have fresh air to breathe, and if the roof didn't cave in, or there wasn't another slide, or a sudden storm didn't clog the shaft with snow, or a hundred other disasters didn't occur to make their tenuous position any more fragile, they'd be okay for a while. He closed his eyes, feeling every tired muscle in his arms and shoulders. For the time being they were safe, and he was too tired to worry about all the rest right now.

He reached up to pull off his ski cap, only to have his shoulder cramp painfully. It was a familiar soreness. The injury that had ended his football career troubled him from time to time. He groaned loudly.

"Are you all right?" Maggie asked.

"Just a muscle spasm." He winced, trying without much success to massage the sore spot.

"Here, I can do that," she offered, rising up onto her knees.

"You don't have to. It'll be all right."

"No, really," she insisted, taking off her gloves. The small tunnel of light linking them to the outside world made her feel enormously better. She felt less trapped, less abandoned, and she was ready to burst with gratitude. "Besides, it's the least I can do. You worked so hard." She motioned to his jacket. "Here, take that off."

Kyle shrugged, then unzipped his parka and slid it off his shoulders. "If you're sure you don't mind."

For Maggie it wasn't a matter of minding or not minding. The fact was she felt a little awkward and embarrassed at the thought of putting her hands on his broad, straight shoulders. It was such a familiar gesture for two strangers, but she thought she owed him something. After all, besides saving her life, he'd expended a monumental effort tunneling the air passage through the snow. The very least she could do was lend him the benefit of her two free hands.

Her hands felt clumsy and stiff at first—almost as stiff and tense as the taut muscles she felt through Kyle's bulky ski sweater. She timidly massaged the area where he'd indicated, gradually gaining more confidence as she felt the tension in his shoulders easing.

Had she noticed just how broad his shoulders were before? She knew all about his career as a football player, but as a quarterback he didn't exactly fit into the standard thick-necked football-player stereotype. Actually, he looked anything but. Whenever she'd seen him in court or during legal conferences, he'd always worn a dark, conservative business suit or sport coat and slacks.

Of course, like any other woman who saw him, she'd made note of the fact that he was rather nice-looking. She didn't doubt there were plenty of women who found that kind of hazel-eyed, sandy-haired, all-American Robert Redford look of his very appealing, though it was hardly her type. But had she ever really noticed just how much strength there was in that lean, muscular frame of his? Had it ever caught her attention just how firm and solid his shoulders really were? He didn't have that "buffed up" look like those muscle-bound giants she saw at the gym. So how had she happened to miss the power and the muscle that were there?

Her hands pressed deep, stroking the muscles from shoulder to neck, coaxing out the tension and soothing away the pain. Closing her eyes, she thought of the strength it had taken to push that rusted pipe skyward, of the toll it had taken on him. She massaged and stroked, wishing there were no bulky sweater or cotton turtleneck in the way. How would it feel to run her hands along those hard, ample arms? What would it be like to feel the strength of them around her—touching, holding, caressing?

"Is this how you worked your way through law school?"

"Hmm— What?" Maggie's eyes flew open and she snatched her hands away from his shoulders as though she'd been burned. What in heaven's name had she been thinking? Color rose in her face when she remembered the picture of him she'd had in her mind. "What was that?"

"Giving massages?" Kyle repeated. "You do it like a pro."

"Oh, no," Maggie murmured, shaking her head vehemently. She slid down to her bottom and leaned back against the wall. At that moment, she was actually grateful for the near darkness. Her cheeks flamed with embarrassment. "Strictly amateur status."

He chuckled softly, remembering. "I swear, some of the masseuses they sent us when I played for the Blues took pleasure in seeing how miserable they could make you." He sensed her sudden awkwardness and hesitated. "Well...uh...it felt great. Thanks."

Her silence disturbed him. She'd surprised him when she'd offered to rub out his shoulder. It had been a rather considerate thing for her to do, and he'd come to think of her as a barracuda, devoid of feelings. Consideration wasn't something he was used to getting from Margaret Danner, attorney-at-law. In fact, he'd almost convinced himself the woman actually took pleasure in making him squirm.

She'd certainly lived up to everything he'd ever heard about her—tough, ruthless, tenacious. Cindy couldn't have found anyone better to look out for her interests. But, then, Cindy hadn't really needed any help. She'd known all along she had the power to make him do what she wanted; he just hadn't wanted to believe she'd actually use it.

He'd been wrong.

He touched his shoulder that had cramped up earlier. He'd meant it when he'd said she'd massaged him like a pro. His muscles felt much better now, and he'd appreciated the gesture she'd made. Apparently Miss Danner wasn't completely without feelings.

Kyle remembered the first time he'd seen her. He'd been waiting for Steven on the steps outside the Sacramento County Courthouse when he'd caught sight of a woman walking toward him. Tall, slender and with that shiny brown shoulder-length hair and dark, chocolate-brown eyes, she'd just about captured the attention of every man in a ten-block radius. The thought that this could be the infamous man-eating lady lawyer he'd heard his ex-wife had hired had never entered his mind. By her reputation alone, he'd expected Margaret Danner to look like a cross between a line backer and the bride of Frankenstein. The woman who'd captured his attention on the steps that day had been about as far from either of those as one could imagine.

It was obvious that she hadn't known who he was at that moment, either, for when she passed him, she'd looked up and smiled at him. Kyle had remembered that smile; it had nearly taken his breath. Of course, once they'd met face-to-face in the courtroom and she'd realized who he was, she'd never looked at him that way again.

And smiling had been out of the question.

Kyle stood and slid his parka up over his shoulders. It was getting dark, and the dim light from the air shaft was starting to disappear. He picked up the dis-

posable lighter from the floor and flicked the flame to
life.

"I think I'll take a look around here. See what we've
got," he said, turning to Maggie. "It looks like we
might be stuck for the night."

Chapter Two

Kyle began a slow, careful search of their small vault. The cabin really wasn't much of a cabin at all. It was more of a one-room shack, dusty and rundown. In a dark corner there was a rotting mattress with a filthy sleeping bag strewn upon it.

Reaching down, Kyle picked up the end of the mattress and the deteriorating fabric broke off in his hand. Beneath the mattress, though, he found a heavy plastic tarp, and there was a rusted coffeepot and a few small half-burned candles lying beside it. After lighting one of the small candles, he snuffed out the flame of the lighter and returned it to his pocket. Its remaining fuel was their only source of fire, and they had to start conserving it.

He slid the mattress and tarp across the floor to where Maggie sat. As meager as they were, these few provisions just might be enough to save their lives—at least for a while.

"You found a candle?"

"A couple of them," he said, handing her the burning candle along with the others. "Just small ones."

"These are great," she said, coming slowly to her feet.

"I found this, too," he said, holding up the rusted coffeepot. "We can melt snow in here. At least have some drinking water."

Maggie eyed the rusted pot with distaste and wondered if she'd ever get that thirsty. "What is this place, anyway? Someone couldn't have lived here, could they?"

Kyle glanced around again. "Actually, I think the ski-lift operators used to use it but—" He stopped and gave the mattress a kick, waving away the dust that billowed up. "There hasn't been anyone around in a long time. The old ski lift used to run along here. The lodge shut it down when the new one was built a few years ago and they turned this run into a snowmobile and cross-country trail. It probably hasn't been used since then." Suddenly remembering, he patted the inside pocket of his parka. Reaching inside, he pulled out three small granola bars. "Oh, I forgot about these."

"Wonderful." Maggie laughed, smiling up at him. "You're amazing."

He looked at her, an odd, quizzical expression on his face. He'd suddenly felt ridiculously embarrassed by her offhanded compliment. "I—uh, forgot I'd grabbed them this morning."

"Wait a minute," Maggie said excitedly, searching her own pocket. She pulled out a half-eaten roll of candy mints. Guiltily, she remembered having popped several of the mints into her mouth as she'd listened to instructions from the snowmobile operator at the lodge earlier. As she looked down at the remaining roll, that innocent act suddenly seemed unforgivably frivolous. Handing the roll to Kyle, she shrugged with regret. "I forgot I'd eaten some earlier. Sorry."

Kyle surveyed their pitiful supplies. They would help. The sleeping bag would help them keep warm, the mattress and plastic tarp would keep them off the frozen floor and the candles would give them some light. And with the candy mints and granola bars, they wouldn't starve—at least not for a while. But the simple fact remained, if help didn't arrive soon, they were going to be in real trouble.

He turned and looked at Maggie, who was quietly eyeing their dubious stock of supplies. There had been such hope in her expression when he'd shown her the candles. The reflection of that small flame had danced in her dark eyes, and foolishly he'd found that it had pleased him to be able to bring her some comfort, however meager. It was a stupid reaction, he knew. He didn't even like the woman. Why should he care if she was frightened?

But for some ridiculous reason, he felt protective of her. It was absurd, really, probably some weird throwback to the caveman days. This was a tough, hard-nosed lady lawyer. She hardly needed his protection. And yet he'd been gratified to see the enthusiasm in those brown eyes of hers. It beat the hell out of the fear he'd seen in them earlier.

Of course, he tried to tell himself his motives were strictly selfish and self-serving. After all, having her hysterical and frantic wouldn't exactly make things pleasant for him. He was certain she had no idea just how bleak their situation really was, and what did it hurt for him to help her remain optimistic? It kept her quiet and it helped him to think. Besides, she was a smart lady. She'd realize soon enough just how perilous things were.

Still, he'd feel a lot better if he could forget how his heart had tripped in his chest when she'd looked up at him and smiled. It had been just like that day on the courthouse steps, and somehow he had a feeling this smile today was another one he wasn't going to forget.

Maggie sat back down and watched the yellow flame on top of the candle flicker and dance. It was amazing, she thought, just how much light one lone flame could throw. She remembered the awful blackness right after the avalanche, and shuddered again. At least the candlelight had a way of making the small cabin feel less like a tomb.

She didn't relish the thought of spending an entire night trapped in this icy little chamber, but if it couldn't be helped, it couldn't be helped. While Kyle had been exploring the cabin, she'd kept a quiet vigil at the air shaft, expecting any moment to hear sounds from up above, listening for some sign that they were going to be rescued, that help was on its way. She kept telling herself things like this—searches and rescues—took time. It had to be determined they were missing, people would be questioned, answers had to be arrived at. Then search teams would have to be organized, their courses charted and agreed upon—all that required time. There was little they could do in the meantime but wait and hope.

Somehow the hours of the day had passed. There had been long periods where they'd merely sat in silence—waiting, listening for any sound, any indication that they'd been found. But surprisingly, there were also times when they talked.

Maggie was amazed at how easy Kyle was to talk to. Of course, never for a moment did she let her guard down. After all, he was still the man who abused women and neglected children, and she kept him well within the range of her vision at all times—just in case. Still, there were those times, as they sat visiting like amiable acquaintances, when she found herself almost forgetting who he was.

They'd chatted about the weather, their work, and what had brought them to the Winter Haven Lodge for the weekend. It was fairly superficial stuff, but it helped pass the time, and Maggie found herself grateful for that. Kyle would get up periodically and check out the stovepipe to make sure it was clear and open. He would then wait...and listen...but no sound had come.

Maggie found herself watching him, but sometimes she forgot it was because she didn't trust him. Sometimes it was because she actually found herself fascinated. He seemed to be such a stark contrast to what she'd expected. Before today things concerning Kyle Gentry had been pretty black and white for her. He was a jerk—enough said. But now...well, now she wasn't so sure.

She turned as once again he crossed the room and checked the stovepipe. But this time, before returning, he reached up and pulled down a handful of snow. She didn't like having to depend on someone like him, but all and all she had to admit he'd been a pretty capable companion throughout the day. She'd thought he'd gone a little overboard when he'd insisted on tunneling the passage with the stovepipe to ensure them a fresh supply of air. She had hoped they would be rescued long before their air supply became critical, but since it was taking longer than she'd expected, she had to admit his air shaft had come in handy.

Kyle put the handful of snow into the coffeepot and reached for the candle she held. Maggie watched as he proceeded to melt the snow inside the pot with the small flame.

Just like a regular Boy Scout, she thought cynically. At the moment she couldn't help but notice he looked nothing like the bastard who had cheated on his wife and ignored his son. He looked like a curious little boy experimenting with a chemistry set. She had to marvel at the diversity of the man, though. If nothing else, he was resourceful. He'd not only ensured their air passage, thoroughly examined the cabin and its contents and provided them with a source of light, he'd even managed to come prepared with his own granola bars. Was he usually this ingenious, or was this just a one-time shot, one of those quirky examples of stress under fire? Of an old pro coming through when the chips were down?

It had to be a fluke, she decided almost immediately, trying to ignore how the candlelight softened the rugged features of his face. It had to be. He was just a dumb jock who'd gotten lucky. He hardly struck her as the ingenious type, and from everything Cindy had told her, he was neither well-intentioned nor kind.

"Here," he said, sitting down next to her and offering her the coffeepot. "Have some water."

"You mean it worked?" Maggie asked, peering into the pot at the murky liquid at the bottom.

"Of course it worked. Try some."

Maggie looked at the thick rust on the rim of the pot and shook her head. "No, thanks." She handed the pot back to him. "You first."

"Oh, go ahead," he urged, offering her the pot again. "I insist."

Maggie glanced down at the pot, then back to Kyle, and shook her head again. "No, no, that's okay. Help yourself."

"Sure?"

"Absolutely," she replied, thinking she'd probably never been so sure of anything in her life.

Shrugging, Kyle gingerly put the pot to his lips and tilted it back. Closing his eyes, he swallowed with a gulp, then lowered the pot back down.

"Well?" Maggie prompted, watching as though she expected him to transform or something.

"Well what?"

"Well, how was it?"

"It was water," he said noncommittally, noticing for the first time just how thick her lashes were. "Very *cold* water I might add."

"How did it taste?"

Kyle thought for a moment about the odd mixture of liquid and floating particles he'd forced himself to swallow and a small shiver made him wince just a little. "Gritty."

There was one, brief moment when they stared into each other's eyes in the faint candlelight. Then a small, thin smile began to soften the hard lines of his face and Maggie felt her lips begin to twitch.

Maybe it was because their situation was so grave, but never had laughter felt so sweet. Kyle leaned back, holding his sides, and roared. Maggie buried her head in her hand, tears forming in her eyes and rolling down her cheeks. It was infectious—one spasm following another. The merest snicker, the smallest chuckle inciting still other attacks, until both were too weak to go on. Exhausted, they collapsed against the hard wall of the cabin.

"I have no idea what was inside that pot last, but I can tell you for certain it wasn't coffee," Kyle gasped wearily, switching to a thick, phony German accent and fighting off another attack of laughter. "And I wouldn't be surprised if I woke up tomorrow and found I'd been transformed into a giant bug."

"Mr. Samsa, I presume? Or shall I just call you 'Gregor'?" Maggie giggled, referring to the famous Kafka character from *Metamorphosis*. She wiped at the tears in her eyes and sighed heavily. The laughter had felt good—wonderful, in fact. It had made her forget for a moment about the cold and the darkness, and left her deliciously weary. The long night ahead seemed much less threatening.

"How about something to eat?" Kyle asked, reaching into his pocket and pulling out one of the granola bars. Breaking it into two pieces, he handed her half.

"Thanks," she said, accepting the bar and taking a bite out of it. "Shall we wash it down with a little melted snow?"

They both smiled, but were too weak for any more laughter, and quietly concentrated on their food. Maggie hadn't realized until that moment just how hungry she was. She'd had only a light breakfast before leaving the lodge this morning. There had been a beautiful breakfast buffet set out, but she hadn't wanted to take the time.

Chewing on the sweet mixture of honey and oats, Maggie thought about the bacon and sausages at the buffet, of the Belgian waffles and scrambled eggs, of the fresh fruits and flaky scones. She could almost smell their aroma, and she salivated. If she'd only had to do it over again . . . She groaned loudly.

"You okay?" Kyle asked.

Maggie nodded, popping the last of the granola bar into her mouth. "Just thinking."

"About what?"

She looked at him and gave a tired laugh. "You don't want to know."

Kyle studied her for a moment. Fatigue was clearly evident in her face and his own muscles were weary with exhaustion. Even though the snow insulated them to some extent, he was certain the temperature had dropped with the arrival of night. He rose to his feet and reached for the sleeping bag. "We should probably think about getting some rest. It's been a rough day."

"*That* has to be the understatement of the year," Maggie mumbled sleepily. She watched as he slid the mattress closer to the wall. "What are you doing?"

"I'm making our bed."

"You're what?" she demanded, wide-awake now.

"I'm getting our bed ready," Kyle said again, finding the exacting tone in her voice a little annoying.

"I'm not sleeping on that thing," she stated flatly, shaking her head. "It's filthy."

"Well, excuse me if the accommodations aren't up to your standards, Miss Danner," he told her with a small, sarcastic laugh. This was the prima donna he'd been expecting to see. "This isn't the Ritz."

Maggie bristled at his sarcasm. This sounded more like the Kyle Gentry she understood. "Regardless. I still don't feel it's necessary to...grovel in the dirt."

"But at least *groveling*—as you so quaintly put it—gets us off the floor. The ground is frozen in case you hadn't noticed."

"It feels fine to me," she told him, making a point of moving to demonstrate her comfort. "You take the mattress if you want. I'll be all right where I am."

"You'll freeze."

"I'll be fine."

"No, you won't."

"Yes, I will," she insisted.

Kyle shook his head. "You're the stubbornest person I've ever met."

"Being stubborn has nothing to do with it."

"Oh, no? Then what would you call it?"

She folded her arms over her chest and gave him a deliberate look. Perhaps it was just as well they got everything out in the open. "You seem to forget, Mr. Gentry, that we're still involved in an adversarial relationship, but I haven't."

"Adversarial relationsh…" His voice trailed off. He couldn't believe what he was hearing. "What the hell does your being Cindy's lawyer have to do with any of this?"

"Surely you must see what an awkward position this puts us in," she pointed out to him reasonably. "And the situation is compromising enough without us sharing the same…the same sleeping accommodations."

Kyle's temper snapped then. "Fine—just *fine*. Do whatever you want." He leaned toward her, pointing an accusing finger. "But get one thing straight. All I'm interested in is survival here—not getting you into bed. But, hey, if you'd rather sit up and freeze that tight ass of yours in order to avoid a possible conflict of interest, I won't stop you." He climbed onto the mattress and pulled the sleeping bag over him like a blanket. "I saved your contentious hide once today. You can bet I won't make that same mistake again."

"Fine," Maggie asserted, a little louder than she'd intended.

"Fine," he answered, flouncing onto his side and stirring up a cloud of dust. He leaned over and blew out the candle, causing the curtain of darkness to immediately descend upon them.

"W-what did you do that for?" she asked in the darkness, trying as best she could to keep the fear from her voice.

"Do what?"

"Blow out the candle."

"Did you expect to leave it burning all night?"

His tone was so caustic that she didn't want to admit that was exactly what she'd wanted to do. Sinking her hands deep into her pockets, she leaned her head back against the hard wall and tightly closed her eyes. She tried not to think about the blackness around her or the loathsome man just a few feet away.

The darkness seemed to magnify even the slightest of sounds—each small rustle of her nylon parka, the catching of her breath in her throat, even the quiet chatter of her teeth. In the inky stillness, each frail movement became the equivalent of an outburst.

She opened her eyes, the surrounding darkness no less black than with them closed. She forced the lids wider and wider, trying desperately to detect even the faintest of shadows or the slightest hint of change. There was none.

She shivered, gooseflesh rising along the skin of her arms despite the billowy insulation of her parka. Damn Kyle Gentry, anyway, she thought as she pulled her hands from her pockets and rubbed at her cold arms in an attempt to warm them up. She was only cold because of him. Surely he understood the power of suggestion. She hadn't even been aware of the frigid temperature and the icy air until all his talk about freezing and having to stay warm. And the darkness only made it feel that much colder.

Slipping her hands back into her pockets, she tried to pull her parka more closely around her. She closed her eyes, striving to push all thought as to where she was or what had happened from her mind. She didn't want to think about that wall of white that had come crashing toward her; she didn't want to remember the sound of its roaring fury, or the many feet of snow that now covered them.

She forced herself to think of her law office, of the cases she had waiting for her, of the work she'd left undone. But despite her best efforts, the cold would not be ignored. A finger of ice slowly made its way up from the floor, seeping through the downy layers of her leggings and parka.

Maybe she had been a little hasty with Gentry's suggestion. Maybe it would have been wiser to have some protection from the frigid ground, despite how foul the conditions. But it was too late to do anything about it now. Frankly, she didn't care how cold it got. She'd prefer to risk freezing to death than to give him the satisfaction of knowing she might have been wrong.

Her teeth began to chatter more vigorously, their movement causing a quaking to resonate through her entire body. She thought about how he would gloat if he were to know just how miserable she was, how he would smirk and scoff at her foolishness, deride her concerns and—

Just then she felt a gloved hand on her arm and her thoughts scattered.

"Look, I know you're uncomfortable. I'm uncomfortable, too," Kyle whispered in the darkness. "But the only hope we have of getting out of here is to stick together."

There was no sarcasm in his tone, no ridiculing, no gloating, and Maggie fought down a hard knot of emotion in her throat. She didn't resist when he took her hand and carefully guided her through the darkness to the mattress.

"Let's get warm," he murmured, pulling her beneath the sleeping bag.

Maggie felt terribly self-conscious lying so close beside him, and at that moment she was grateful the candle was no longer burning. Light would have only made the situation even more embarrassing. But she gloried in the slow warmth that began to spread to her frozen limbs. The mattress smelled rotten and the sleeping bag reeked, but gradually her shivering stopped and those areas where their bodies touched generated a comforting heat.

"Better?" he asked, feeling the tension slowly easing from her.

"B-better," she murmured. He was being so nice, and that merely made her feel all the more foolish.

"I can light the candle for a while if you like?"

She realized then she'd forgotten all about the darkness, and she began to feel uncomfortable for an entirely different reason. In the warmth, with Kyle so close, the awful darkness suddenly didn't seem so bad. Where it had once felt cold and threatening, it now had a warm, restful feel.

"No," she told him after a moment. "It's fine."

She wished he'd stop being so nice to her. It made her uneasy. Why couldn't he just start acting like the bastard Cindy had described him as—selfish, self-indulgent and self-centered. At least she'd know what to expect then.

But the man lying beside her, who shared his warmth and had shown her concern and sensitivity, was none of those things. This man was kind and gentle, and a lot harder to figure out. How did she cope with this man? And how could she ever make herself understand how his kindness and sensitivity made her feel.

"Mr. Gentry—Kyle," she whispered in the darkness. She'd never called him by his given name before, but considering the circumstances, the usual formalities hardly seemed appropriate.

"Yes?"

"I never thanked you."

"My reason's were strictly selfish," he scoffed good-naturedly. "You're making me warmer, too, you know."

"No, not that," she said, finding that being grateful to him didn't feel as uncomfortable as she'd thought it would. "About this morning. If you hadn't been there...if you hadn't dragged me away from the snowmobile..."

"We both got lucky today," he said casually, but the breath paused momentarily in his lungs. "I'm just glad this old cabin was here."

Maggie shook her head. "You saved my life. Thank you."

Kyle released the air from his lungs in a long, slow breath, and tried to ignore the curious pressure he felt in his chest. "Go to sleep."

Long after he felt all of the tension slip from her body and her slow, even breathing signaled her deep sleep, Kyle stared up into the darkness. Just who was this Margaret Danner? He knew for a fact that she'd been making his life miserable for almost two years now with her poking and prodding into his personal and business life, and that his lawyer had told him what a tough adversary she was in the courtroom. But somehow he was having trouble associating the picture of the hard, no-holds-barred tiger lady with the woman who slept so peacefully beside him.

It had surprised him when she'd offered her thanks. He hadn't expected that. Actually, grabbing her and pulling her into the cover of the cabin had been done more out of instinct than anything else. But finding her up on the mountain had been no accident.

He'd seen her take off on the snowmobile from the lodge and had decided to follow on his cross-country skis out of curiosity more than anything else. He still smarted from their encounter when they'd stumbled upon each other in the lobby the night before. She'd been pretty rude to him and that had infuriated him. After all, they weren't total strangers, and they were both adults, both capable of being civil. It wasn't as though he'd expected them to stand around and "chat" like old friends or anything like that. But the look she had given him—so curt, so cool. She'd glared at him as though he were lowest form of life on the planet.

Why had that bothered him so much? She was his ex-wife's lawyer. She'd spent the past year and a half virtually putting the screws to him. Why should he care what she thought of him? But for some reason he still couldn't understand, he did care, and he had started up that mountain determined to confront her.

Just then Maggie stirred sleepily, shifting her weight and tossing a leg casually over the top of his. Kyle smiled to himself. He'd confronted the lady all right— although this wasn't exactly what he'd had in mind. A lot had happened to change things between them in the past twelve hours. A day ago all he had was Margaret Danner's contempt. Now he had her gratitude.

As fatigue made his eyelids heavy and his thoughts haze over, he remembered just how nice it felt to have the weight of that leg resting across his. Yeah, he decided sleepily, his thoughts scattering into the blackness around him, he'd take gratitude over contempt any day.

Chapter Three

Maggie could hardly believe she'd actually fallen asleep. But opening her eyes and staring at the dull, gray light streaming down their narrow air shaft, testified to the fact that the night had passed.

She was only mildly surprised to find herself pinned quite securely beneath one of Kyle's arms, which was draped heavily over the top of her. And she was only a little embarrassed to feel the length of his strong, warm body behind her, pressing tightly against her back. And it disturbed her just a bit when she realized that she rested her head on the hard muscle of his other arm. Apparently, nestled in the warmth between those two strong extremities and in the lee of his sturdy frame, she had slept quite soundly throughout the night.

But she had to admit to being just a little uncomfortable to discover that sometime during the night the two of them had not only maneuvered so closely together, but somehow Kyle's face had become buried in the warm area at the base of her neck. She could, quite literally, feel the roughened texture of his lips along her skin.

Oh, she knew she had to accept the fact that these were extraordinary circumstances, and the ordinary rules governing propriety and good conduct simply didn't apply. Still, the feel of those hard, unyielding lips had been inappropriate in some way, despite the circumstances.

She turned just a little, hoping to roust him enough so that he might move aside just a bit, but the movement only succeeded in making matters worse. Growling sleepily, Kyle stirred. His arms tightened about her, and his face nestled even deeper. But that wasn't the worst of it. As he snuggled himself deeper into her warmth, his lips brushed her neck with what felt like a gentle, sleepy kiss.

Maggie was galvanized by a tumult of sensation. Her body went rigid with surprise and her heart began to pound fiercely in her chest. She felt hot and cold at the same time, and her mouth went sandy dry.

Get hold of yourself, she censured herself. *Maintain a perspective.*

She drew a deep breath into her lungs to help calm her runaway emotions and force her tense muscles to relax. After all, it wasn't as though it had been a real kiss or anything like that. Actually, it—the...uh ...kiss—or whatever it was—had been little more than reflex, little more than a mechanical function of some sort.

But her reasoning did nothing to calm her pounding heart. She realized then that circumstances had nothing to do with her feelings of discomfort. What was inappropriate about the situation was not that they had shared a mattress, that they had slept tangled in each other's arms, or that he had inadvertently brushed a kiss along her neck. What was inappropriate about this whole thing was the way it made her feel.

Kyle Gentry wasn't the kind of man she wanted anything to do with. He wasn't the kind of person to trust your feelings with—feelings of any kind. Caring about someone like him wasn't merely asking for trouble, it was courting disaster. Besides, not only would it be professionally unethical for her, but from everything she'd learned about him from his ex-wife, he was the kind of man a woman should definitely stay away from.

She thought about the gentle kiss he'd positioned on her neck, about the sure, possessive way he still held her and a shiver moved down the length of her spine. Reflex, she reminded herself again. Automatic reflex. He was used to holding a woman in his arms, used to a woman in his bed—many of them, according to Cindy. Was it any wonder he felt at such ease with their position? Sharing his bed with a woman was obviously something he'd become quite accustomed to.

Just then Kyle shifted his weight, his arms closing tightly and clutching her to his chest. She struggled against him, hoping to free herself of his hold before he awoke. Even though the light filtering down the stovepipe was hardly the harsh light of day, it diluted the awful darkness enough to make her uncomfortable about facing him.

As he slept, she carefully eased one heavy arm from her waist, then shifted her weight to one side and reached for the other. But she had no more than touched the hand of his other arm, when he suddenly seemed to spring to life. With a noisy yawn, he stretched his arms and brought them around her again. She did her best, but her struggles seemed only to make matters worse. Like a rag doll, she was tossed and turned, flung to one side and maneuvered about. In the commotion, her cap was knocked loose and her hair tumbled down, covering her face and confusing things even more.

She wasn't sure just how it happened, or how she could correct it, but somehow she managed to find herself sprawled across the top of him. Thinking things couldn't get any more awkward than they already were, she reached up and pushed her hair aside, only to find herself staring straight into his clear hazel eyes.

Kyle stirred, stretching lazily and flexing his stiff, sore muscles. He inhaled deeply, the sweet fragrance filling his senses, making him think of a field of flowers, spring grass and warm balmy nights. He was in that dreamy state between sleep and wakefulness and he savored the warm, comfortable feeling. But the moment was fleeting, as the memory of the snow, the cold, and being trapped brought reality crashing down on his head like twenty feet of new snow. Rolling onto his back, he opened his eyes.

He was still drowsy with sleep, and his mind wouldn't quite compute. For a moment all he could do was stare up into Maggie's startled gaze and wonder if he had ever noticed the delicate flecks of amber that mingled with the brown in her eyes before. Her hair dangled, hitting him on the face and chin. It felt silky and warm, and he forgot about the cold and the ice. He remembered the field of flowers in his dream, and could almost feel the warmth of the sun on his skin.

Her full weight rested on top of him, and with explicit clarity he became aware of the distinctive feel of her—the swell of her breasts, the gentle curve of her hip, the fragile rise of her bottom. Despite the bulky clothing and the unconventional circumstances, that delicate pressure along the length of his supine form was something no man could mistake. It was the unique and singular feel of a woman.

"G-good morning," she mumbled awkwardly, quickly diverting her eyes. She flattened her hands against his chest and attempted to pull herself free.

"Good morning," he murmured. When he realized it was he who prevented her from rising, he promptly released his hold. How had his arms gotten around her? "Oh, sorry."

"No problem," she said, knocking the sleeping bag aside and sitting up. She felt about for her cap, locating it wedged between them. She wasn't sure whether it was the temperature or simply her embarrassment, but it felt much warmer in the cabin than it had the night before.

"Were you able to get much sleep?"

"Hmm— What?" she stammered, unzipping a side pocket in her parka and slipping her cap inside. "Yes. Yes, I was. How about you?"

He nodded, even though in the dim light they could barely see each other. He stretched, feeling the twinges of a night spent in uncomfortable conditions. His shoulder ached, and he thought of the massage she had given him yesterday. "Were you warm enough?"

Maggie thought of how snugly she'd been nestled against him and felt her cheeks grow hot. "Yes. Yes, I was. I slept better than I thought I would." She hesitated a little. "Uh—look...about that thing last night. I acted pretty silly...I guess I was just scared and—"

"Forget it," Kyle said, cutting her off. "We both were a little on edge."

Maggie knew he was being very gracious, and she was grateful. She hated to think about what a fuss she'd made over their sharing the mattress. The man had been concentrating on survival, and she'd acted like an outraged virgin. When she thought of the stupid things she'd said, she wanted to crawl into a hole— one other than the icy one she shared with him. Still, he hadn't mocked or made fun of her, and he'd gracefully accepted her apology. It had been a very kind, generous thing to do. Maybe there was another side to Kyle Gentry that his ex-wife had failed to mention.

Kyle turned slowly, glancing at her profile in the shadowy light. Her hair tumbled to her shoulders, and her neck was long and thin. He thought about what it had felt like to have that soft body of hers atop him and marveled at how much, in the past few hours, his perception of Margaret Danner had changed.

Even before this he'd thought of her as attractive. A woman with her kind of classic good looks was a little hard for a man to ignore. But in the passing of these last, intense hours, he'd come to see her as a puzzling, enigmatic woman. Only it wasn't her complexities he found himself thinking about when he'd awakened to find her wrapped in his arms. Complexities weren't what filled his mind with images when he felt the soft pressure of her long, luscious body pressing against his. And it wasn't the woman's complexities that had his body chemistry singing this very moment.

Desire. Its blow had been clean, and sharp and unexpected.

Kyle sat up, surprised and uncomfortable with his thoughts. The confinement must be getting to him. The last thing he needed was to get all hung up on a woman—*any* woman. But especially this one. Cindy might have used him, but a woman like Margaret Danner would chew a man up and spit him out.

Purposefully, he turned his thoughts to other cravings—like caffeine—and slowly made it to his feet. Stretching his protesting muscles, he reached into his pocket and pulled out another of the granola bars. It was hardly the cup of strong, black coffee his body cried out for, but he knew they were lucky to have anything at all.

"Breakfast?" he asked, breaking the bar and offering her half.

"Thanks," Maggie said, reaching up and taking it from him. She stepped off the mattress, getting to her feet and dusting herself off. Peering carefully about the place, she turned back to him. "Did we ever decide where the bathroom was?"

"Well, there had been something like one in that small closet over there," he said, pointing into the darkness. "But I'm afraid the plumbing is long gone. Not much more than a pit left now. The dirt's exposed, but we can use it. Want me to light a candle?"

"Thanks." Maggie nodded, wondering how many other indignities she'd be forced to suffer before all of this was over.

"Be careful where you step," he warned, handing her the small wedge of wax. "There are some large cracks and holes in the floor."

"Oh, fine," Maggie muttered, carefully making her way across the room.

"And watch out for spiders."

"Great," she muttered again.

"Black widows."

"Black widows?" she shrieked, whirling back around and nearly snuffing the flame. Maybe she didn't have to go that badly after all.

Kyle held in a snicker. "Just a precaution. They'd probably be moving awfully slow in this kind of weather, but it wouldn't hurt to keep an eye open, anyway."

"Black widows," Maggie mumbled, easing around and fumbling her way back through the darkness. She cautiously stepped into the fetid closet that had once housed the toilet, grousing to herself. "Why don't I just keep an eye out for a rat or two while I'm at it?"

"That probably wouldn't be a bad idea," Kyle called to her from the mattress.

She heard his mischievous laughter from around the corner and groaned loudly. She went about her business as expeditiously as possible, thinking any moment something slithery, or crawly or completely disgusting would appear out of the gloom. After she had finished, she hurriedly made her way back across the broken floor and sat down on the mattress. But when Kyle reached for the candle to make his own journey to that same dark closet, she looked up at him.

"Be careful not to step on the rat," she said drolly, popping the last of her half of the granola bar into her mouth. "He was rather big, but had such cute little brown eyes."

She almost giggled when she saw him stop and turn around. Served him right, she thought, with all his talk of spiders. But even in the gloomy light of the cabin, she could see his quirky smile.

"Big one you say? Hmm," He thought for a moment. "Sounds like fresh meat for dinner tonight."

"Oh, yuck!" Maggie choked, crumpling the granola wrapper and tossing it at him.

"Never try and tease a teaser." He chuckled as he disappeared around the dark corner.

A teaser. Was that how he'd describe himself? she wondered. From what she'd observed of the man the term seemed to apply. It seemed to fit the easygoing nature and sense of humor. But it was a far cry from the picture Cindy had painted. Just when did teasing become torment?

The time seemed to pass. Because the sports watch that Kyle wore around his wrist had been smashed sometime during their escape from the avalanche, it was impossible for them to know what time of the day it was. But even without a clock, Maggie was aware of the passage of time. One hour slowly followed the other, and they were left with little to do but wait.

When it appeared that the light filtering in from the air shaft had begun to dwindle and fade they noticed immediately. True, the time was passing slowly, but it couldn't have been more than midday. There was no way the sun could be going down.

Kyle looked through the pipe to the small patch of sky it allowed. Where the narrow shaft had been filled with brilliant blue sky earlier in the morning, it now showed only gloomy gray clouds.

"Looks like another storm building," Kyle said.

"What does that mean?"

"More snow." He shrugged. "It'll probably get colder."

Maggie glanced up at the dimming light of the air shaft. She remembered the weather report she'd listened to on the drive up the mountain the other night. Snow storms predicted. Winter warnings. Use caution. Chains required.

It grew darker in the cabin, and with the darkness came the cold. Kyle walked back to the mattress and sat down again. "Warm enough? We can pull up the sleeping bag."

"No," Maggie whispered, thinking in her life she'd never forget the musty smell of that filthy thing.

"Hey, don't look so worried," he told her, smiling and bumping her with his shoulder. "It'll be okay."

"It'll take longer now, won't it?" she asked grimly. "The storm will slow the rescuers."

"It could," he admitted. The storm made him uneasy, too. The rafters of this old cabin wouldn't be able to take much more. Enough snow and the whole place could come crashing down like a house of cards. And Maggie was right. Another storm didn't speak well of their chances for rescue. At best it could delay it—using up precious time they didn't have. And at worse... well, that wasn't something he was ready to think about yet. So for both their sakes, he forced himself to remain optimistic. "But we're protected. We'll keep warm. You've heard of the igloo effect. We'll be all right. Besides," he added, scooting around on the mattress so that he could lean back against the wall, "you know how unpredictable things can be around here. The weather changes constantly. This thing is liable to blow right over the top of us."

Maggie nodded slowly, but the feelings of fear and dread were hard to ignore. The light from the air shaft grew fainter and fainter, and the wind sweeping down it felt bitter and cold.

They both fell silent, quietly watching as the cabin grew darker and darker. The wind above must have picked up, because it whistled down the shaft, sending small clots of snow and soot along with it. Periodically, Kyle would get up and check the pipe, making sure it remained unplugged. He wished now that he'd held on to his ski poles. They would have come in handy keeping the pipe clear. Unfortunately, he'd dropped them somewhere along the way, and now they were no doubt beneath a few tons of snow.

He glanced down at the cracked and broken stove, bending to pick up one of the smashed pieces.

"Gosh, I wish Conner was here," he said, turning the piece around and looking at the charred, rusted underbelly. "He'd find some way to piece this thing together and get it working again. He loves putting things together." He glanced about the dark cabin, then tossed the chunk of stove back down with the others. "What am I saying? I don't want him here."

Maggie looked up. She was surprised to hear him mention his eight-year-old son. According to Cindy, he rarely ever did. "He's with his mother this weekend?"

"Yeah," Kyle muttered, walking back to the mattress. "I'd hoped to bring him with me, but Cindy changed her mind at the last minute." His expression was grim as he slowly shook his head. "I'm grateful now that she did."

"I met him once—Conner. He's a nice little boy."

"Thanks. He really is." Kyle smiled, leaning back against the wall again. Slowly the smile faded. "The divorce was hard on him, though." He turned to her then. "But I guess you see a lot of that in your line of work."

"Too much, I'm afraid."

"I'll never forget the look in his eyes the first time I told him about it—the split, I mean. Damn." He sighed heavily, thinking back. "Talk about second thoughts. I told Cindy I was tempted to just forget the whole thing—anything to avoid putting him through that."

Back out? Had she heard him right? Cindy had never mentioned anything about second thoughts or backing out. According to her, Kyle had just walked out one day without so much as a backward glance.

"But all that arguing wasn't good for him, either," Kyle went on. "I don't know, maybe I'm just trying to make myself feel better, but I still think it's worked out for the better. We see each other all the time, so that hasn't really changed. He's at my place most weekends, and we have Scout meetings every Wednesday night."

"Scouts?" Maggie almost choked.

"Yeah," he said, eyeing her skeptically. "Why?"

"No reason." She shrugged. "It's just—you're a Scout?"

He raised a brow and gave her his best indignant look. "You find that so difficult to believe?"

"Well...I mean, come on. You? That is a little hard to believe."

"Madam, you wound me," he said, clutching at his chest. "I fear my reputation has been much maligned."

His teasing, lighthearted sense of humor still surprised her. After the picture Cindy had painted of him, she just never would have suspected it of him. She couldn't help laughing. "I'm sorry. It just surprised me, that's all."

"Well, if you find that so amusing, I'm almost afraid to tell you the rest," he added dryly.

"The rest?"

"Well, please, try and contain yourself," he requested, giving her another skeptical look. "But I also happen to be the den leader."

An image appeared in her head, and she started to giggle. "You don't mean you're the guy with the Bermuda shorts and Smokey the Bear hat, do you?"

"All right, enough of that."

"And the whistle and the clipboard?"

"Okay, okay."

"And the knee socks?"

"Isn't there an ambulance you should be chasing or something?" But he laughed as hard as she.

"No, really," she said after a while, sagging heavily against the wall. The laughter had gone, but the good feeling remained. "I think that's wonderful."

"Oh, right," he scoffed.

"No, honestly," she said, waving off the laughter.

"Well, it gives us something special to share between us—guy stuff, you know. And it helps me to get to know and keep in touch with some of his friends and their fathers," he said. "Do the camping, cookout, sleep under the stars thing—stuff like that."

"Conner must love it," Maggie said, having to admit all this took her by surprise.

"I think he does—at least I hope he does. Otherwise I'm putting myself through a lot of pain for nothing. We went to the annual father-son camp out last month and had a great time."

"Sounds like you two are expert campers."

"You got that right." Kyle smiled, remembering. "And next year I'll even bet we'll make it through the entire night without the tent falling in on us."

"It didn't."

"Oh, yes. Yes, it did," he assured her. "But hey, no big deal. It only rained once during the night."

"Oh, no, you must have gotten soaked."

"Not that it mattered," he added quickly. "We just hopped into the showers in the morning."

She was almost afraid to ask, beginning to understand the tenor of the trip. "No hot water?"

"You know," he told her thoughtfully. "I bet if you stood under that ice water long enough even this place would feel warm."

Maggie shook her head. "What a disaster."

"The camping trip from hell," he told her carefully, but his face softened and his smile widened. "But Conner had the time of his life. That's all that was important."

She regarded him for a moment. "You sound like a good dad."

"I love my kid." He shrugged. "After that, I'm just feeling my way along like everyone else."

They fell silent then, and Maggie became caught up in her thoughts. The way Cindy had described it, Kyle rarely took time for his son, and saw the child as little more than a nuisance. But listening to him, hearing about the Scouting and the camping, he sounded every bit the proud, involved parent. She began to wonder what else Cindy Gentry had neglected to mention about her ex-husband.

The day seemed to drag on forever. The gloom in the small cabin grew almost unbearable. Maggie became restless. Standing, she marched across the room and glared up at the somber gray sky, then turned around and stomped back to the mattress.

"How can you stand it?" she asked, frustrated. Sitting back down, she turned to Kyle and raised her hand helplessly. "Just sitting here. I swear, these wall are closing in on me."

Kyle reached into his pocket and pulled out the candy mints. For the first time he felt really hungry, and the half granola bar earlier had offered little relief. Pulling off his gloves, he tore the paper down on the roll and offered one to Maggie first.

"No, thanks," she said, but her voice cracked with emotion.

"Go on, take one," he urged, reaching up hesitantly and stroking an errant lock of hair back from her face. Her hair felt as warm and as silky as he'd imagined. "It'll make you feel better."

Maggie dutifully took one of the mints and slipped it between her lips. Its sharp, clean bite felt almost as cold as the air outside.

Kyle regarded her carefully. He understood her frustration and anxiety. He felt much the same way. Despair was something they were going to have to deal with the longer they were trapped, and she was feeling pretty desperate now. She needed comforting, solace, and normally those were things he felt awkward offering to women. But Maggie wasn't really like other women, and these weren't normal conditions.

Reaching his arm out, he slowly picked up her hand and held it.

"Thanks," she murmured, taking immense comfort in the small gesture. "I'm sorry to act like such a ninny. It's just...just..." Emotion twisted in her throat. She didn't want to cry—she really didn't. It solved nothing, and it made her look so weak.

Lifting his free arm and slipping it around her shoulders had been a purely instinctive move. Apparently, when it came to Maggie Danner, all the old hang-ups and precautions simply didn't apply.

"I know," he whispered. "You're frustrated, angry. Me, too."

"If there was just something we could do," she said helplessly, leaning her head back against his arm and looking out into the murky grayness of the cabin. "Some way we could let them know where we are."

"We're doing all we should, all we can," he assured her, empathizing with the agony in her voice. "The most important thing we can do is to save our strength, stay warm and dry and wait."

"It's the waiting..."

"It's hard, I know," he said, giving her a little squeeze. "But we'll make it."

She turned and gave him a small smile. One, lone tear dropped from her lash onto her cheek and began slowly rolling down. Carefully, Kyle reached over and wiped the tear away, his finger pausing on her cheek and stroking slowly along her jaw.

She was so beautiful, and her eyes were so full of pain. He wanted nothing more at that moment than to take her into his arms, to hold her and protect her and take away all the pain. His finger drifted to her chin, tilting it upward, lifting it to him, even as his face drew nearer.

Maggie watched in fascination as his face moved closer and closer. Looking up into his clear hazel eyes, she felt as though she'd suddenly stepped out of herself. They were no longer in that icy cabin, trapped beneath many feet of snow. Somehow they'd been transported—to a place that was warm, and secure—where there were no clients, no law suits, no conflicts and no scandal—where there was no place for danger, no call for restraint and no time for doubts.

Kyle felt an ache deep inside, a yearning that was rooted somewhere very near to his soul. Maggie's lips parted slightly, and he wanted nothing more than to taste and exult in them. He hovered just a breath away, like a starving man savoring the sweet agony before indulgence, close enough so that he could all but feel their silky touch.

"Maggie," he murmured unsteadily, brushing her lips once, twice. The ache inside him had escalated to hunger, and hunger to need. But just as he bent to kiss her fully, a terrible sound had them both pulling back in shock and confusion.

The floor beneath them rumbled and swayed. Then, in a suddenly flurry of motion and sound, the cabin was thrown into total darkness.

Chapter Four

Kyle fumbled in the darkness, finding the lighter in his pocket and pulling it out. Igniting the flame, he searched the floor for a candle.

"What is it?" Maggie asked frantically. "What's happening?"

"Another slide," he mumbled, standing to light two of the small candles he found beside the mattress. He bent down and handed one to her. "Stay here."

He found his way to the stovepipe, holding the candle high to provide as much light as possible. After a moment, he extinguished the flame and tossed the candle to the floor.

Maggie got down on her knees, holding her candle as though it were her only life line. The rumbling beneath them had stopped, the only noise in the cabin now came from Kyle at the stovepipe. She could see his dark silhouette, and from the sounds she could tell he struggled and worked with the pipe. It seemed as though the seconds dragged on forever, but finally, after a clamor, light came streaming down the shaft once again.

Maggie realized then she'd been holding her breath, and emptied her lungs with one long sigh. "What was it?"

"A rock," Kyle said, dusting himself off and bending to find the intruding object. He picked it up along with the candle he'd tossed, then walked back across the room and handed her the rock. "It jammed the pipe."

Maggie studied the stone. It seemed so harmless in her hand, not much more than a few inches in diameter, and yet it served to reinforce to her just how meager and fragile their link to the outside was. "You said there was another slide?"

"Up the mountain, I think," he said, brushing the last of the snow and soot from his parka. He sat back down on the mattress and looked at the rock in her hand. "Save it—a paperweight for your desk, maybe. Something to help you remember the trip."

"I don't think I'll have any trouble remembering all of this," she remarked dryly.

She casually glanced up at him, and found herself staring into his clear, brown eyes. Immediately she remembered the sweet, warm, magical place those eyes had taken her to just before calamity had struck. For that one incredible moment it had been wonderful to be in that special place with him, but thinking about it now made her flustered and embarrassed, and she quickly looked away. No, she thought, she wasn't going to need any souvenirs to help her remember this trip—or this man.

"Uh . . . you think it's over then," she asked stiffly, absently putting the stone into her pocket. "The slide, I mean."

"I think so," he said, wishing like hell he could be half as sure as he sounded. He didn't know how much more this little cabin would take before it self-destructed, and there was no way to know just how perilous their situation really was.

He slid back and leaned against the wall. He watched as she fussed with her gloves, then nervously pulled out her cap and slipped it back onto her head. He sensed her discomfort, and knew the reason for it.

He'd kissed her—not a real honest-to-God kiss, maybe, but close enough. He'd actually done little more than brush her lips with his, but it had been enough to give him a feel for her, a sample of her taste, of her passion and desire. There had been a hint of the mint on her lips, and he could feel its coolness in his mouth even now.

That damn little rock had come very close to destroying their tenuous air supply. He would have to remember to keep a better watch on the shaft from now on. But thinking about her lips—of how they'd felt, how they'd tasted—made him want to forget all about air supplies, and darkness and avalanches.

He wondered for a moment what might have happened if that damn rock hadn't elected that precise instant to become wedged in the pipe. Would she have actually allowed him to kiss her? Would she have let him sink his mouth to hers? Would she have let him part her lips and taste the warm, rich flavor of her? And if she would have let him kiss her, would he still be kissing her now?

Heat surged through his body at the thought of them kissing. But, as she would say in her profession, the point was now moot. The moment was gone, and there would be no going back. She might have been willing to let him touch her a moment ago, but it was obvious she was having some serious second thoughts now.

He thought of trying to say something light and casual about what had happened, something teasing and funny that would put her mind to rest, that would let her know he wasn't taking any of this too seriously, but he couldn't bring himself to do it. He couldn't make light of something when the unvarnished truth of the matter was he did take it seriously—very seriously.

But it was better this way, he thought as he watched her trying to tuck her long hair back up into the confines of the cap. Just let it go, let it die a quiet, uneventful death. After all, neither of them was exactly in a position to think straight. She was vulnerable and frightened, and he was...

Kyle shook his head. *He* was the real prize, that's what he was. He'd been acting like a star-struck kid on his first date rather than a man trapped and fighting for his life. He was actually enjoying the fact that she needed him, that she'd come to look to him for her survival. He liked it that she'd come to think better of him. Maybe that was what had made him start up this mountain after her in the first place. He knew what a low opinion she had of him, and for some ridiculous reason he'd wanted to change all that. He'd wanted her to see him in a different light, to get to know him, to... like him.

Gentry, you're such an idiot, he told himself darkly. He'd been parading around like some kind of half-wit high-school quarterback intent on impressing the new girl in class.

He glanced up at her as she struggled with her hair, her movements shaky and unsteady. Well, he'd impressed her, all right. He'd impressed her so much that she was so self-conscious and ill at ease she could hardly look at him. She was trying very hard to act as though nothing had happened, as though being kissed by her client's ex-husband was something that happened all the time, that it was nothing to be concerned about.

Good job, stupid, he cursed himself angrily. *You've got a real talent when it comes to women. I'll bet even if you tried real hard you couldn't make her feel more embarrassed.*

What he would do was follow her lead. He'd do her a favor and let the whole thing drop, forget about it, try to pretend that it never happened. He owed her that much. Besides, if they ever got out of here—and that was becoming a bigger and bigger if—but *if* by some miracle they were rescued, reality could pack a very harsh punch. Sooner or later they would end up facing each other from opposite sides of a courtroom or conference table and that would not only prove to be embarrassing, but almost impossible.

* * *

Maggie paused and drew in a deep breath. If she didn't stop trembling, she'd never get the stupid hair to stay inside the cap. If Kyle would only *do* something—anything—just as long as he'd stop staring at her.

What could she have been thinking? Had she lost her mind? Had the confinement and the snow and the lack of food caused her to go completely mad? Wasn't it enough that she'd woken up this morning practically glued to his side? Wasn't it enough that she'd had to sleep on the same filthy mattress, beneath the same rotting sleeping bag, with him? Hadn't she compromised herself enough? How could she have let him . . . *kiss* her?

Every time she thought about it, every time she thought how caught up she'd become, how mesmerized she'd been, how recklessly she'd behaved, she wanted to just shrivel up and disappear. How could she have acted so foolishly?

She understood they were trapped, that time and circumstance had placed them in an awkward situation and that conventional precautions and taboos simply had to be set aside for the sake of survival. But that didn't mean that she had to lose her head completely. Extraordinary circumstances didn't give her license to behave foolishly. She had to start using her head. She had to start thinking rationally and not let her fears and her emotions get in the way.

Kyle Gentry was the ex-husband of a client—period! Case closed. Since terms of the settlement between her client and him had been agreed upon, leaving them only to formalize those agreements, there really was no concern as to a conflict of interest. But the fact remained that propriety and common sense dictated that a certain decorum be maintained. And that decorum did not include his kissing her.

Maggie glanced down at him hesitantly, suddenly uncertain how she was supposed to act. That stupid kiss had changed everything. She felt ridiculously unsure about everything at the moment. Should she stand or should she sit, talk or remain silent, smile or act insulted? She could hardly stand there forever, but if she was to sit, would he take that as an indication that she was interested in picking up where they left off?

She paced about the cabin floor, walking cautiously in the thick, gray light. The movement stimulated her circulation and warded off the cold a bit. But as she paced nervously back and forth, she felt her level of anxiety and awkwardness increasing.

"Maggie."

She jumped at the sound of his voice. "Hmm— What?"

"It's getting colder. Why don't you sit down, cover up for a while? Maybe see if you can get some rest."

Maggie listened to his voice, analyzing every word, studying every nuance, on the alert for any clue that he was suggesting more than his words would indicate. But she heard nothing—no insolence, no double entendre, no veiled invitation. If anything, his tone had sounded vacant, even a little distant. For the first time it occurred to her that he, too, might have some regrets about what had happened.

"Right," she replied, almost under her breath. Crawling back onto the mattress, she pulled the sleeping bag up around her. Perched rigidly on the edge, she kept him in her peripheral vision, almost daring him to make a move.

He made none.

After a while, she felt herself relax. She stole a quick glance in his direction, but he wasn't even looking at her. He was lying on his back, arms bent to cradle his head, and his eyes were closed.

Surely he wasn't sleeping. She stared down at him for a moment longer, then turned away.

Well, evidently that was that, she thought to herself, feeling ridiculously let down. It seemed she'd worried for nothing. There would be no awkward confrontations, no clumsy attempts to explain, no embarrassing scenes. Well, that was quite a relief. How fortunate. What luck. She should feel lucky, relieved, grateful, happy....

Of course she should. So why, then, was she so annoyed?

"You never said if you had any children of your own," he said suddenly.

She almost jumped at the sound of his voice, but she had to admit it made her feel a little better. Apparently she hadn't put him to sleep after all, despite the fact that his eyes still remained closed. "What? Why?"

He opened his eyes then and looked up at her. "Just making conversation. I'm having just a little trouble thinking about anything except how empty my stomach is. I thought a little conversation would take my mind off it. Do you mind?"

"Uh—no, I don't mind," she said, shaking her head. "And no, I don't—have children, I mean."

"Not married?"

"No."

"Not now or haven't yet?"

She smiled just a little. "Haven't yet and never will."

"Never? That sounds awfully definite. Why's that?" he asked, coming up on an elbow.

"You forget what I do for a living. Believe me, when you see as many bad marriages as I do, you don't exactly find yourself looking forward to the experience."

"I see. So is this something all divorce lawyers feel, or is this just your own conclusion?"

"Well, I can only speak for myself, but I would bet there are a fair number who feel the way I do."

"But that seems so unfair, doesn't it? I mean, you only see those marriages that have failed."

"Are there any other kind?"

He shook his head and laid it back down. "That sounds awfully cynical."

"Occupational hazard."

He paused for a moment, then continued. "So, it's your career that's turned you off marriage, then?"

"Among other things."

"Oh? Other things? Such as?"

"Such as I'm the product of a broken home," Maggie said after a moment. Her childhood wasn't a topic she enjoyed discussing. "Statistics aren't good for children of broken homes."

"Statistics aren't all that much better for children from traditional homes, either, so what does that prove?"

"It proves my case. Marriage is a risky proposition, even under the best of circumstances."

Kyle rose on his elbow and looked up at her. He wasn't entirely comfortable being put in the position of defending marriage, especially given his track record, but for some reason it bothered him to hear her knock it. "God, you really are jaded."

"Not jaded, just realistic."

"I think you need a break from divorce court for a while. It's distorting your outlook. Marriages can work, you know."

"Oh, and this comes from the voice of experience?" That had been a low blow, but it had been out of her mouth before she'd had time to stop it.

He bristled just a little. "Okay, my marriage failed, I admit it. But that doesn't mean I won't try again."

"So you just intend to keep trying until you get it right, is that it?"

"No," he said slowly, purposefully ignoring his anger. "I intend to be much more careful the next time around." He laid back down and closed his eyes again. "So what does your boyfriend think of your warped opinion of marriage? Or does he know?"

"I haven't had a 'boyfriend' since I was in high school," Maggie informed him brusquely, pulling the sleeping bag up a little farther. "But if you're referring to the men I see, I don't really see what difference it should make to them."

Them. He thought about that for a moment. That would indicate more than one. Just how many men did she keep on a string? "It wouldn't make a difference to them to know you're not interested in marriage?"

"No, it wouldn't," she insisted, then hedged a little. "Besides, they're not...those kinds of relationships."

"There's no one *special* in your life, then?"

"Is there anyone *special* in yours?" she asked back, avoiding the question.

He glanced up at her and smiled purposefully. "We were talking about you."

"Having trouble narrowing it down to one?"

He gave her a deliberate look. "That sounds like something Cindy would say."

"And you're avoiding the question."

"Okay, okay," he conceded gracefully. "I've got nothing to hide. If you must know, there's been no one special in my life for a very long time."

"So is that to mean you prefer to play the field?"

"Something like that."

"Well, which is it? Like that, or something else?"

He looked up at her again, remembering how much he hated the penchant of lawyers to play games with precision of wording. "Actually, Miss Danner, I haven't been playing much of anything to be exact— field or otherwise."

"Oh, right."

"You don't believe me?"

"No."

"Why, because Cindy told you about the long line of women I kept?"

"Oh, no, you don't," she said, shaking her head emphatically. "I never discuss what my clients tell me."

"You don't have to. I know my ex-wife," he mumbled. He knew all too well the stories Cindy liked to tell. His former wife had a very convenient talent for rewriting the past. What stories had she told Maggie, and just how much of them had Maggie believed? Was that why she'd had such a low opinion of him? "But we were, as I recall, discussing you and your...ah, *men* friends. Sounds like you're pretty good at playing the field yourself."

"I see a few friends," she hedged.

"No strings? No ties that bind?"

"Not at the moment," she told him, sounding more defensive than she'd have liked. Of course, she failed to mention the times she'd been accused of sabotaging her relationships in order to avoid any permanent commitment.

"And your rather thorny views on marriage have never bothered any of them?"

"I don't know—I never asked them. Look," she said finally, growing impatient. "What's with all the questions? Why are you so interested?"

"Just curious," he said easily. "You know a lot about me. You've been poking and prodding into my life for almost two years now. But I know hardly anything about you. I want to know how a nice girl from Sacramento becomes a hotshot divorce lawyer and ends up with such a jaded view of marriage, that's all."

"I'd rather not talk about it."

"Why?"

"I just don't."

"Afraid of something?"

"No, I'm not afraid of anything."

"Then why won't you tell me?"

"Because it's none of your business. Can we talk about something else?"

"I want to talk about this. You've piqued my curiosity. Wasn't there ever a time when you wanted to get married?"

"Drop it, Gentry."

"I mean, I thought all little girls grew up dreaming of their wedding days."

"Well, maybe they do," she conceded, wanting all this to stop. She threw off the sleeping bag and climbed to her feet. "But not all of us had a lot of time to dream when we were kids."

Kyle sat up slowly. Her tone had been sarcastic, but he'd heard the pain in her voice and it had pierced him like a hot knife in the chest. There had been a serious edge to the conversation from the beginning, but he'd just thought it had been from pent-up emotions and feelings of awkwardness left over from the kiss. He'd never intended to hurt her. "Look, I didn't mean—"

"Oh, no. You want all the grisly details. I'll give them to you. I don't mind. It's not a terribly interesting story, nothing that hasn't happened a hundred times before to a hundred other kids. It's just that when your father walks out on you, leaves your

mother to work two jobs trying to keep a roof over
your head, when you and your sister and three brothers are forced to live in a one-room apartment and
work after school jobs because your father doesn't
bother sending his support payments—well, let's just
say your picture of marriage can become a little tar-
nished.''

''Maggie, I'm sorry.''

''Forget it,'' she said, taking a deep breath and
waving off his concern with a careless gesture. ''But
you want to hear the real clincher in all of this? Four
years after he left, I found out he'd moved back to
Sacramento. He came into the restaurant where I
waited tables after school. That's how I found out
about his new wife and baby. He didn't even recognize me, but when they left, I followed them home.
They lived in a beautiful house—picket fence, two cars
parked in the drive—you get the picture.'' She stopped
for a moment and let out a humorless laugh. ''I remember watching him carry his baby into the house
and thinking how my sister, Terri Lynn, and I used to
make up stories about how great everything was going to be when Daddy came back, how he was going
to take care of us, make everything all right.'' She
shook her head. ''All the time he'd been living on the
other side of town in his new house with his new family. He'd tossed us away and we never even knew it.''

Kyle studied her carefully, feeling a piece of the
puzzle that had become Margaret Danner fall into
place. ''So you went into family law to make sure what
happened to your family wouldn't happen to any one
else.''

"Oh, please, don't make it sound so noble." She glared at him. Insight wasn't something she wanted from him at the moment, especially since he'd hit so close to the mark.

"But it is rather noble," he said quietly, thinking about that sad little girl and how betrayed she must have felt by the father she loved. That little girl said a lot about the woman today.

"There's nothing noble about it," she snapped. What was she doing? Why was she telling him about all of this? She hated dredging up all those old, painful memories, and the last thing she wanted from him was pity. In fact, she didn't want anything from him. "I merely get what's fair and equitable for my clients."

"Oh? Is that what you did for Cindy?"

Maggie stopped abruptly and looked back at him. She knew there was nothing fair or equitable in the arrangement he'd agreed to sign for his ex-wife. And there certainly had been nothing noble in demanding it.

Kyle watched her from the mattress. The rigid set of her shoulders, the nervous clenching of her hands, the restless pacing sent a clear message. He'd hit a nerve.

Maggie stalked to the air shaft and looked up. High above, the sliver of gray sky appeared dark and ominous, and she felt unsettled and uneasy. The walls were closing in again, and she felt restless and jumpy. What was happening to her? When had she lost control? When had everything gotten so out of hand, and so confusing? It seemed she could no more manage the conversation than she could control the way she felt.

It was as though everything had suddenly begun to feel oppressive—the cabin, the cold, the darkness . . . and the man.

Just then there was another small tremor beneath them, a low, slow vibration. The rafters above creaked and groaned, and a flurry of snow fell down from the pipe. Somewhere above them, another avalanche had made its way catastrophically down the mountain.

"Damn it, I can't stand it," Maggie said finally, all the emotions she'd managed to wall up for the past twenty-four hours spilling out like the wall of snow down the mountain. "I can't stand it. Where are they? Why haven't they found us?" She turned to the air passage, her fists clenched at her side. "We're down here, damn you," she cried, screaming up the narrow pipe. "Why can't you find us?"

"Maggie," Kyle said quietly, coming off the mattress and crossing the room to her. He grabbed her by the upper arms and turned her to him. "Maggie, don't."

"They're not coming are they," she said to him, tears streaming down her face. "We're just going to stay down here forever, aren't we? We're going to die down here, down here in the dark."

"Maggie, now stop!" he demanded, giving her a stern shake. He didn't want to hear this, didn't want her to even think it.

"Where are you?" she shouted again, her voice boarding on hysterical. Pulling free of his hold, she screamed up the stovepipe. "Don't you know we're down here?"

Her sudden outburst surprised him, but he understood it. The fear, the monotony, the uncertainty had tensions mounting. He pulled her toward him, but she struggled and fought against him.

"How can you stand it?" she demanded. "How can you stand to just sit here and do nothing? How can you stand to just wait to die?"

"Maggie," he murmured again, pulling her into his arms. Seeing her like this tore at him. This latest tremor had been the last straw. Her frail hold on hope had snapped, and reality had brought with it desperation and fear. She struggled against his embrace, but he held her firm, held her until her struggles had become sobs and her curses had turned to cries.

She couldn't lose hope; he wouldn't let her. It had been like a game they played—by reassuring her, it had been easier for him to believe; by keeping up her spirits, his also remained heightened. He couldn't let despair and fear destroy the delicate balance of their game. There had to be a way—there just had to be. He had to do something for her and for himself.

They'd waited long enough. More than twenty-four hours had passed since the avalanche, and they were no closer to getting out than they were a day ago. They couldn't go on forever. The temperatures were freezing and the storm remained severe. They had waited for a sign of rescue, for any evidence that help was on the way, but they had waited long enough. It was time to face the fact that they were on their own, and one way or another, he was going to find a way to get them out.

"Maggie," he whispered as he helped her back to the mattress. "I want you to lie down for a while. I want you to rest."

Maggie let him guide her down onto the mattress. Her emotional outburst had left her spent. She lay back, watching as he unzipped his parka. Covering her with it, he turned and walked to the closed cabin door.

The door had jammed and stuck during the slide, making it impossible to move. But now Kyle labored and worked at the hinges, using his hands and fingers until he could wiggle and loosen the stubborn joints.

"What are you doing?" Maggie asked, lifting up on an elbow.

"I'm going to try—" His words stopped abruptly as he pitted the considerable strength of his shoulders against the roughed wooden slats of the door "—to get this thing—" he shifted his weight, edging the heavy wooden door up and away from the frame "—off."

He lifted the door cautiously to one side, revealing a carefully constructed wall of snow that stretched from floor to ceiling. Packed tight, it remained in place even with the door gone, hanging within the doorframe like a large, oversize piece of art.

"What did you do that for?" Maggie asked, sitting up and tossing off the parka.

Bending, he picked up the rusted coffeepot and turned back to her. "I'm going to dig us out."

Chapter Five

"You're going to what?" Maggie asked, getting up off the mattress and walking toward him.

"I'm going to dig us out," he repeated, turning back to the wall of snow and scooping out a piece of it with the coffeepot. "See?"

Maggie regarded him for a long moment. "Why are you doing this?"

"Why not?" he asked glibly, dumping the snow in the coffeepot onto the floor and turning for another.

"Kyle."

"Go lie down, Maggie," he insisted, moving around her and continuing his work.

"Kyle," she said again, reaching out and grabbing his arm, forcing him to stop.

He looked down at her, and a sharp, constricting pain tightened in his chest. "You were right, Maggie. We can't just sit here and wait."

He slipped his arm free and turned back to his work. Maggie stood and watched as he quietly labored away. She forgot about how afraid she'd been, forgot about the restlessness and monotony that had caused her to become so emotional, forgot about the close quarters and bleak circumstances. With each mass of snow he removed from that chalky wall of white, she felt herself imbued with new hope and enthusiasm.

"I've got an idea," she said suddenly, fumbling back across the cabin to the air shaft. She rummaged through the clutter and found the wobbly firewood box that Kyle had used yesterday to stand on while struggling with the stovepipe. She picked it up and carried it to the door. "If you put the snow in here, I can haul it to the corner and start a pile over there. Get it out of the way."

Kyle looked at her. The panic had all but vanished from her eyes, and in its place there was an eager, almost excited look. He felt that strange, constricting pressure in his chest again—like the one he'd felt when he'd held her earlier. Cool, competent Margaret Danner, attorney-at-law, didn't need anything from anyone. But he was finding the woman with him had a very different side to her. Maybe Margaret was tough and invulnerable, but Maggie could be hurt and frightened, she could touch and be touched and she could look at a man with those large, sad eyes of hers and make him want to do all he could to have her smile again.

In a million years he never would have believed that beneath that tough, uncompromising exterior of assurance and certainty, he'd find the soul of a sensitive, vulnerable woman. He could never reach out to someone like Margaret Danner, but Maggie...Maggie was a different story. He could reach out to Maggie, he could make those sad eyes of hers dance, he could hold her and comfort her and he could wipe away her tears. But the most important thing he'd discovered was he could give her hope.

He didn't want to think about all the reasons motivating him, or this growing desire he had to shield and protect her. He didn't know what the chances were of him successfully digging them out. The job was cold, strenuous and painstakingly slow. But he knew that the look of promise and hope in her soft brown eyes was worth any hardship, and made him willing to die trying.

They labored for the rest of the afternoon, until the cold and the darkness forced them to stop. Their progress had been slow, but Kyle had managed to burrow the start of a small tunnel out from the cabin upward toward the surface.

Having finished for the night, Kyle leaned the heavy door back against its frame. His body heavy from exhaustion, he stumbled to the mattress and fumbled for his parka. Finding it, he slipped it over his strained and tired shoulders and pushed his lifeless arms into the sleeves.

Even though he had used the coffeepot to cut and scrape out the snow, his hands had become wet and frosty cold. His gloves had offered some protection, but since they had been damaged yesterday from the sharp edge of the stovepipe, the cold and the moisture had penetrated. Numb and nearly useless, his fingers struggled with his zipper.

Maggie quickly rushed to help. She zipped up the parka and reached into his pocket for the lighter.

"If there was just something around here we could burn," she moaned, lighting one of the candles. "A small fire would help warm your hands."

"They'll be all right," Kyle insisted, rubbing them together over the small flame of the candle. "Besides, there isn't anything. I looked earlier."

"What about the wood box?" she asked, pointing to the box she'd used to haul the snow into the corner.

"How would you get it started? We don't have anything to kindle it. Besides, the wood's too wet now."

"I suppose you're right," Maggie mumbled. After a moment, she pulled off her gloves. "Here, put these on."

"Maggie, they won't fit," Kyle pointed out, shaking his head. "I'm fine, really."

But Maggie looked unconvinced. She was worried about him. The hard work had taken its toll on him. He'd toiled tirelessly for hours, backbreaking labor that had drained and depleted his strength. His face looked ashen and deep lines of exhaustion marred the rugged features. His lips were tinged with a pale shade of blue and his eyes appeared fixed and glassy. She brought him a handful of clean, white snow and made him eat some, despite his feeble protests.

"Not exactly the steak and baked potato I'd been hoping for," he murmured, wetting his lips with the snow and falling back onto the mattress. "Where is that damn room service when you really need it?"

"It's right here," she said tightly, finding the last granola bar. The fact that he was able to maintain his sense of humor in these miserable conditions touched at something in her, and she quickly had to blink back the sting of tears. "And might I say we have something delightful on the menu tonight." She pulled the wrapper back and broke the granola bar in half. "A lovely little collection of oats and nuts, joined together in a sweet, honey glaze. How does that sound?"

"Actually, it sounds great," he replied honestly, salivating. Sitting up, he pulled his cold hand from his pocket and took the half bar that she offered. He ate it hungrily, its small proportion not nearly enough to fill the gaping void in his empty stomach.

Maggie watched as he wolfed down his half of the granola bar, and glanced at her untouched half. "You know, I'm really not hungry," she lied, ignoring her cramping stomach. "Why don't you take this."

Kyle stopped and looked at her, thinking he'd never heard quite such a sweet lie in his life—or had ever appreciated one so much before. He reached over and with one finger stroked the length of her cheek. Even with the impaired feeling in his hands, he was aware of the warmth and the softness of her skin.

"You worked hard today," he pointed out. "It's important you keep up your strength, too."

Maggie felt a thick knot of emotion in her throat. There was something so genuine in his eyes, so sincere, something that had her wanting to reach out and soothe away all the hurt and all the anguish. There was a kindness to this man, a kindness Cindy Gentry had either ignored or forgotten about.

A rush of frigid wind suddenly blew down the air shaft, bringing a flurry of snowflakes with it. The candle flickered wildly, nearly blowing out.

"The temperature is dropping," Maggie announced in a flat tone.

Kyle braced himself against the chill. "Can you tell if it's snowing?"

Maggie peered up the shaft and shook her head. "I don't think so. Why?"

"Just curious." He shrugged, neglecting to mention his concern about more snow creating a greater danger of a cave-in and the risk of the air shaft clogging again.

"Do you think it'll get much colder tonight?"

Kyle shivered again. "A few degrees one way or the other won't matter."

Maggie turned to him and laughed a little. "Such an optimist. Is there any situation you don't find a silver lining in?"

"Sure, plenty," he said, taking his hands from his pockets and rubbing them together. " I just don't think concentrating on the dark side ever helps. Just get in there and make the most of what you got."

"Now, that sounds suspiciously like something a football coach might have once said."

Kyle smiled, thinking she was probably right. "Don't laugh, you can learn a lot from football."

"Oh, right. Push 'em back, push 'em back—stuff like that."

"Now, why do I get the impression you don't think too much of football players?" he asked dryly.

"I don't know what you're talking about. I've always adored men with fifty-inch necks."

"Okay, that's it," he teased, threatening to come up off the mattress after her. But the sudden, severe cramping in his shoulder had him wincing and falling back.

"Your shoulder again?"

"Yeah," he mumbled, rubbing it. "A little reminder from one of your thick-necked friends."

Maggie absently slipped the granola bar into her pocket and moved around the mattress to reach for his shoulder. Through his thick parka, she slowly massaged the tender area. She felt none of the awkwardness or discomfort she'd experienced the day before. Now it seemed like the most natural of things to do.

"How did you get started in football, anyway? Were you a jock in high school?"

"You bet." He smiled proudly. "Lettered in football, dated the head cheerleader, won a full scholarship. I sort of went, you'll forgive the expression, the whole nine yards."

"Not to mention being chosen all-American in college, first-choice draft pick to the pros and one of the highest paid quarterbacks in the history of the game," she continued for him. She smiled when he looked up at her, surprised. "Well, I have had almost two years to do my homework. And now you're a successful businessman. Would you say you attribute your success to the wholesome philosophies you learned on the playing field?"

"No," he said simply, ignoring her sarcasm and groaning just a little as the strained muscles eased beneath her touch. "I attribute it to luck. I was just lucky to have been born able to throw a football."

"You must like the game an awful lot to give it so much credit."

"It wasn't a matter of liking or disliking it. Football was all I had."

"Oh, come on, all you had? Isn't that just a little strong?"

"Is it? It's the truth."

"It's a game Kyle. How could a *game* make that much difference in a person's life?"

"It makes a difference when it's the only chance you're given. For me it wasn't a question of if I liked it or not—I was good at it. And for a kid like me that was important." He paused, letting the gentle motion of her hands lull him. "My folks didn't have anything. It was all they could do to make ends meet. There was no way they could have sent my brothers and me to college. But football was something I could do, something I was good at, and it gave me that opportunity." He shrugged, thinking with satisfaction that indirectly it had helped his brothers as well by providing him with the means to pay their tuition. "The pros were just an added bonus, the gravy. More than I could have hoped for. It was enough that I made it to the university."

"And the pros came after that?"

"Yeah, after graduation I played six years for the Sacramento Blues." His eyelids were growing heavy and his tired muscles relaxed. "I hate to sound like a cliché but . . .'' He looked up at her and smiled, giving her his best jock impression. ''Football has been very good to me.''

''I think you're getting punchy,'' she said, giving his shoulder a playful whack.

''I think you may be right,'' he agreed.

Maggie gave his shoulder one last rub, then moved back to the other side of the mattress. Maybe it was just her imagination, but the cabin seemed colder and more desolate. Despite Kyle's optimism about the difference a few degrees of temperature made, the air seemed to have a harsher, more bitter feel. She pulled her jacket around her tighter, trying not to think about the cold wind plummeting down the shaft, or the white plume that appeared every time she spoke or exhaled.

''Doesn't that wind seem to be blowing a lot stronger than usual?'' she asked uneasily.

''I hadn't noticed.'' He shrugged. ''There always seems to be a pretty good wind through this pass.''

She turned and regarded him. ''Is that true, or are you just trying to make me feel better again?''

''Maggie, you're getting paranoid.'' He smiled, wondering how many other times she'd been able to see right through his efforts to console her. ''Weather can often be treacherous in this area.''

''I know. I'm sorry.'' She shrugged. Maybe she was getting paranoid. Another blast whistled down the pipe, causing her to shudder and make a face. ''It just sounds so spooky tonight.''

''Spooky,'' he repeated quietly. He leaned across the mattress toward her and whispered in her ear. ''Well, you realize where we are, don't you?''

"What?" she asked dubiously. "Where?"

"Donner Pass," he said meaningfully, then slowly raised one eyebrow.

"Donner Pass?" she repeated, shaking her head. "I don't get it?"

"Donner Pass?" he prompted again, giving her a conspiratorial wink. "Get it now? *Donner?*"

"Donner, okay." She looked puzzled, and shook her head once more. "What about it?"

"You've never heard of the Donner party?" he asked, referring to the ill-fated 1846 wagon train of California-bound immigrants who became trapped in the Sierras by rugged snowstorms.

"Okay, okay," she groaned, realizing he'd gotten her again with his teasing.

"You know," he told her melodramatically, leaning in closer, "that happened right in this area."

"Kyle."

"And they say sometimes, at night, when the wind blows—"

"I'm not listening," she informed him, making a point to focus her attention elsewhere.

"Well, they say you can still hear—" He stopped suddenly, sitting up and turning his head. After a moment he looked at her. "Did you hear anything?"

"Very funny, very funny," she repeated as he struggled to keep the smile from his face. Her tone was decidedly sarcastic, but she found his teasing strangely endearing. Even as weary and exhausted as he was, he worked to keep her spirits up. "You've had your little joke. Now, can we move on to something else?"

Kyle grinned broadly, liking the bemused exasperation in her eyes. He shrugged innocently. "Just thought you'd like to know, because of all those rumors...well, you know, about how after they ran out of food, they...well, you know."

"Oh! For heaven's sake Kyle," she admonished, remembering the infamous stories of cannibalism associated with the Donner party.

"Just thought you'd want to know, in case you have any ideas," he warned, shifting his weight back against the mattress, "I'll be sleeping with one eye open."

"Oh, go to sleep," she ordered him irritably. "You look terrible."

"You know," he mumbled drowsily. "You're going to have to stop showering me with compliments. It'll go to my head."

Maggie reached for the sleeping bag and waited until Kyle had settled back on the mattress. Even in the faint candlelight, she could see that their bantering had drained him of what little strength he had left. After blowing out the candle, she settled back and drew the sleeping bag over the top of them.

She rested in the darkness, listening to the wind and letting her imagination wander. The sporadic gusts down the stovepipe whistled and moaned, and in her tired mind she could almost hear the sad, lamenting cries from those lonely souls lost in this same treacherous mountain pass more than a century ago.

She thought back over the day. Had it only been this morning when she'd awakened in Kyle's arms? Could only twenty-four hours have passed since she'd last lain in the darkness and let her thoughts wander? It was as though time had shifted and changed, adhering to its own eccentric sort of tempo. Hours passing sluggishly one to the other at one moment, flying by the next, while still making it difficult for her to think back to a time when snow and survival hadn't been the foremost thing in her mind.

Beside her, she felt Kyle's muscular frame. There was so much about the man she still didn't understand, so much that still remained a mystery, and yet there was so much that she had learned.

His love for his son was certain and steadfast, she was convinced of that. She knew Cindy had painted a very different portrait of father and son, but she'd seen Kyle's face when he'd talked about Conner, when he'd told of the camping and the Scouting and the love. Maggie knew divorce distorted images and misconstrued truths, and maybe Cindy's bitterness over all of the other injustices she'd suffered at the hands of this man had made it impossible for her to recognize the truth any longer. But the truth was there nonetheless, and it was evident that Kyle Gentry loved his son and he derived great pleasure in being a father.

She thought about the camping trip he'd told her about with the crumpling tent and the rainstorms, and the cold showers. She smiled to herself, remembering how he'd called it the camping trip from hell. But she bet that to Conner, it had been nothing short of heaven. How many times had she seen divorce end or greatly reduce the father's involvement with his children? The sad irony being that the arguments, the jealousy, the petty disagreements between the divorced couple so often worked to erode the parent-child relationship at a time when a child needed them both the most.

Her thoughts drifted to her own father and the disappointments and hurt she and her sister and brothers had endured. What had ever possessed her to tell Kyle Gentry about all of that? Talking about anything private was something she just didn't normally do, but it seemed that since she'd become trapped in this cabin, she was doing a lot of things she didn't normally do. Like allowing her emotions to get the best of her and sharing a brief kiss with the ex-husband of one of her clients.

She thought back on how soft and soothing his voice had sounded and how it had made her feel. She remembered the look in his eyes and gentle feel of his lips. Sharing secrets about a painful childhood had been one thing, but that kiss had been something else entirely. Was it simply the bleakness of their situation or the underlying fear and uncertainty of what was going to happen to them that had her reacting to him so, or was it something else? How was she to tell? And would she ever be given a chance to find out?

She thought of the image she'd once had of him, of the Kyle Gentry described to her by Cindy and the one she'd put together in her mind. It seemed impossible to reconcile that image with the man she'd shared these long, dark hours with. He'd been a strong, able and thoughtful companion to her during their ordeal. She hadn't started out wanting to admire or commend him for his strength and sensitivity, but she grudgingly had to admit now that she did. She also hadn't forgotten that she owed him her life.

For eighteen long months she'd thought of him as her nemesis, as the enemy on the other side of the courtroom. She'd wanted him to pay for the misery he'd caused, for the brutality and abuse he'd inflicted on his wife and son. But now she was having a difficult time adapting all those old thoughts and feelings with what she knew and what she'd come to understand about the man.

She understood better his love for his son. If Cindy had seen abuse or neglect, it wasn't there now. And the giant portion of wealth and resources Maggie had demanded for her client and that she'd fought so hard to secure had been the result of Kyle's own drive and initiative. Nothing had been handed to him on a silver platter—he'd had to work long and hard to accomplish what he had.

The avalanche had done more than threaten her life. It had confused everything. All those things she'd been so certain of, everything that had seemed so crystal clear, so black-and-white, so cut-and-dried only a few short days ago, were now mired in doubt and uncertainty. Was it just that their small, buried cabin had become lost in time and space, isolated from the rest of the world and reality that had her stepping back and taking a second look? She'd always told herself that every case she handled had two sides, but she didn't think she'd truly understood just what that meant—until now.

Kyle's sudden, fierce shiver had her thoughts scattering and brought her back to the moment with a start. She realized then that she felt no warmth radiating from him. Instead, his whole body quaked steadily, shivering with cold.

He'd said nothing to her, no complaints, no grievances, but Maggie suspected his hands still suffered from the cold. She remembered her own foolishness last night when she'd tried to weather the icy temperatures, how insidious the cold had been, spreading through her entire body—frigid and deadly.

So much had changed since that wall of snow had trapped them. Kyle Gentry may not have been a perfect husband, but he wasn't exactly the monster she'd thought he was, either. He'd comforted her when she'd needed it and he'd worked to keep her spirits up. Two days ago she might not have considered him worthy of either her time or her attention, but tonight he'd become the focus of both. Sliding closer, she reached out and wrapped her arms around him.

"Your hands," she whispered, pulling off her gloves and feeling his icy skin in the darkness. "They're freezing."

"Damn things," he cursed, the violence of his shivers making his voice jagged. "I can't seem to warm them up."

Maggie pulled the sleeping bag more securely about them, shifting her weight against him until their bodies pressed tightly together. Then, very carefully, she reached for his hands and guided them slowly beneath the layers of her parka and ski sweater to the healing warmth of her bare midriff.

The feel of his frosty hands along her warm skin sent a chill through her entire body, though she'd braced herself for the shock. Instinctively, his hands sought her warmth. When she'd adjusted to their frigid touch, she relaxed her tense muscles and wrapped her arms about him, squeezing tight. Gradually, a soothing heat began to replace the deathly chill, and both their bodies surrendered to it.

Kyle lay in Maggie's arms and thought about the woman who held him so tightly. He knew she felt an obligation to him because he'd saved her life, but did she have any idea how she had saved him? Did she know what her generosity and her caress had meant to him? The cold had been miserable, and his body had been unable to ward off its menacing chill alone. He was exhausted, his muscles weak and drained, and he'd honestly thought he might die.

But no longer. Warmth was spreading through him, infusing him with new life and making him feel better than he had since all this had begun. His hands along her satiny skin were slowly awakening, bringing awareness and sensation back. The feel of her, the warmth of her, the texture of her skin all joined together to fill his mind and senses with her—with Maggie.

Maggie Danner. He said her name to himself over and over again in his mind, liking the sound and the feel of it in his head and in his brain. He felt dizzy and giddy and deliriously content. He knew it was crazy, he knew it made no sense, but in that moment, as her touch and her scent filled his senses, Maggie Danner had become everything to him—life, breath, survival and hope.

He closed his eyes tightly, letting his hands drift just a trifle along her skin. He could hardly remember the hard-fighting lady lawyer who'd made his life miserable for so long. She seemed part of his distant past, long ago and far away. That woman had nothing to do with Maggie, nothing to do with the woman who held him, who comforted him, who had reached out in the darkness and saved him from an icy death.

He knew she'd been embarrassed by her emotional outbursts today. She'd seen them as a sure sign of her weakness and inability to cope. But he'd seen something else entirely. There was nothing weak or incompetent about the woman. But to a little girl who tried very hard not to cry for the father she missed, to a little girl who had tried to be strong and tried to comfort her smaller siblings, tears and emotions were an unpardonable offense.

"Maggie," he whispered as the darkness turned from cold to comfort. "Thank you."

Chapter Six

Kyle drifted slowly back, hovering for a moment in that ethereal area between sleep and consciousness. He felt warm and content, and his dreams had been filled with sunshine and laughter and . . . Maggie.

He felt her stir beside him and his arms tightened around her. His hands were no longer dead and useless from the cold. They had become alive again and he reveled in the feel of every warm, satiny curve, every soft, gentle bend. From somewhere outside the boundaries of this hazy place, he felt the bite of cold and the insinuation of something evil and darkly sinister, but he was too safe, too protected in this nebulous dream place for worry to penetrate.

If he could just stay in this place, this cheerful, enchanted place, with Maggie in his arms and hope in his heart, he believed he could be a happy man—and he hadn't been happy for a very long time. It seemed that for as long as he could remember there had been the uncertainty, there had been the doubts and there had been the danger of Cindy's threats hanging over his head.

He felt himself smiling or maybe it was just another part of the dream. But it didn't matter. He was content to just relax and enjoy. Only, as he moved to shift his weight, the sharp pain that echoed through his shoulder and bolted down his arm had the breath catching in his lungs and brought an abrupt trip to reality. With reality came realization and with realization came the bleak and dismal morning.

"Are you okay?" Maggie mumbled sleepily after hearing him groan.

"Okay," he moaned, straightening his stiff, sore arms. Every muscle protested as he pulled slowly away. Only then did he realize what he'd thought was a dream hadn't been a dream at all. He'd been holding Maggie close. But even more surprising was learning that she still held him, as well.

Reluctantly he pulled back, his sore muscles opposing even the slightest movement. Lying flat on his back, he stared toward the ceiling, only in the heavy gloom of the morning the beams remained shrouded in darkness. He didn't need a news report to tell him the weather outside had grown worse. He'd held little hope of rescue from the very beginning, but now their situation seemed all but hopeless. Had there been any chance that Winter Haven Lodge been spared the slide, rescue teams would have no doubt found them by now, despite the bad weather.

They were starting their third day in the cabin, their third day with no heat, no food and a dwindling hope. They had been lucky so far. They'd managed to keep warm enough virtually by their body heat alone, and they'd been fortunate to be spared the pain of frostbite so far. But that couldn't last forever. Things were going to be a lot more unpleasant from now on.

It was beginning to look more and more as if the tunnel was their best hope to get out, and he prayed he had enough strength left to make it to the surface. His whole body ached and he was feeling the effects of days with essentially no nourishment. Digging through that snow required energy and his was nearly at an end.

But he had to try. Not to try would be to accept death, and he would never do that. He had to try—for himself, for Maggie and for Conner.

Kyle thought of his eight-year-old son and a knot of emotion formed in his throat. He couldn't believe he would never see Conner's dancing eyes and crooked smile again. That he'd never hear his giggle or hear him call him "Pop" again.

Kyle knew Conner was a strong little boy—despite the divorce, despite all the conditions and stipulations it had placed upon him, even despite Cindy's erratic and volatile nature. But could Conner manage without him? Could he cope with the loss and could he go on? He knew his son had come to rely on him for strength, for security and for love. But would memories be enough to pull him through?

"Is everything all right?"

Maggie's question startled him and he jumped. Batting away the moisture that blurred the vision in his eyes, he quickly looked away.

"I'm fine," he said stiffly, sitting up and swinging his legs to the floor. "Fine."

Maggie watched him as he hastily got to his feet. It was still quite dark in the cabin, but she could have sworn his eyes had been shiny with tears. "How do you feel? How are your hands?"

"They're fine," he mumbled, ignoring the complaints from his aching, throbbing muscles. He had a picture of Conner in his head, of his smiling face and laughing eyes. And he still remembered how he'd felt waking up with Maggie in his arms. Those two images were like a signal light in his brain, a beacon guiding him and charting the way. They represented life and living and all that was worth having. He wasn't going to let this cabin become his tomb. One way or another they were getting out of here. They couldn't die. There was simply too much to live for.

He crossed the cabin to the heavy door balanced against the open doorway. Despite the throbbing in his shoulder, he lifted the door away to expose their meager tunnel.

"What are you doing?" Maggie asked. He seemed so distant, so different, not like himself at all.

"I have to start to work," he said simply.

"But, Kyle," she protested, standing up and stepping off the mattress. Her muscles protested loudly, she could only imagine how his felt. "It's so early. You must be still exhausted from yesterday."

"I'm fine."

"Why don't you try and get a little more rest?"

"I'm not tired."

"But, Kyle, don't—"

"Look, Maggie," he said, cutting her off. He didn't want to talk; he didn't even feel comfortable looking at her. She was relying on him, just like Conner, and he couldn't face letting her down. "If you're still tired, lie down and go back to sleep. I've got work to do and I don't have time to stand around and answer a lot of questions."

He turned back to the door and slipped on his damp, ripped gloves. They felt clammy and cold, and for a moment he remembered that awful, deathly chill from the night before. But he couldn't think about that now. What was important now was to dig, while he still had strength and he still had time.

Maggie stood and stared at him, bewildered. Had she missed something? Had something happened during the night she didn't know about? He hadn't acted like this before—driven and distant. Suddenly the man was a stranger. How many sides did he have? Just when she thought she was coming to know him, he made her feel like a stranger again.

She watched as he tore into his work, abrading the solidly packed snow. He'd become a man driven—like a crusader on a divine mission who dared not dally along the way. What had happened during the night to make him react so? Had there been some kind of premonition, some sign of trouble? Did he know something she didn't?

She didn't understand what had happened, but she understood he wasn't in the mood to talk about it. She slowly bent to pick up the wooden fire box, then walked to the door and began to help.

They labored away for several hours in silence, the work tedious and their progress slow. The snow was packed tight, compacted by the sheer weight of itself and it made their job that much harder. Dense and solid, it took tremendous strength to burrow through it.

Maggie dragged boxful after boxful of snow across the rough cabin floor to the corner. By midmorning, a massive pile had formed and began spreading farther and farther. As it amassed, it slowly but surely made the air in the cabin even colder. The size and the volume of snow were almost overwhelming, and she began to wonder what they would do with it all. How much more snow would they have to pull from the tunnel before they reached the surface?

Her arms and legs protested the backbreaking work, but she struggled on. She would occasionally glance over at Kyle but said nothing more to him. He hadn't even so much as looked at her but continued to work with a single-mindedness that seemed to consume him completely. He didn't smile, he didn't tease, he didn't talk, he didn't stop and she began to think he didn't even seem to feel the cold and discomfort.

It remained dreary and dark in the cabin, which made their working all the more difficult. After long hours of toil, Kyle finally stopped, frustrated and depleted.

"Damn it!"

"What is it?" Maggie asked, startled by his sudden outburst. She dumped the last load of snow onto the pile and turned to look at him. "What's the matter?"

"This damn thing," he muttered, holding the coffeepot up for her to see. It was terribly bent and its handle had all but collapsed on itself. "It just isn't working." He thought for a moment, then glanced across the room to where she stood. "Let me see that."

He grabbed the wooden box from Maggie's exhausted arms and examined it carefully.

"What are you going to do?" she asked, becoming impatient with his stony silence.

"Maybe I can use this," he mumbled, setting the box down and bringing his foot down hard against it.

"What did you do that for?" Maggie demanded as the slats of the box gave way with a scream.

He knelt and examined the slats of the broken box carefully.

"Kyle?" Maggie prompted quietly when he failed to answer her.

He pulled a number of the slats loose from what remained of the frame, and tested the strength of several of the them by pressing his weight against them.

"Kyle," Maggie said, prodding him once more, a little louder this time.

Kyle measured several of the slats, picking two that were the closest in length, and rose quickly to his feet.

"Kyle!" she said again. When he pushed past her and started back for the tunnel, her jaw nearly dropped. What was the guy's problem? Had she suddenly become invisible? Even though her arms were weak with exhaustion, she grabbed his arm and spun him back. "All right, that's enough. What's going on here?"

"What are you talking about?"

"You know damn well what I'm talking about," she said. Her anger exploded, and she pushed against his broad chest with the palms of both her hands. "*This*. This silent treatment you've been giving me. Where'd that come from?"

"I don't know what you're talking about," he said testily, trying to push past her.

"You know exactly what I'm talking about," she insisted, stopping him by grabbing an arm of his parka. "Just who do you think you are? Why are you doing this?"

"Maggie, I don't have time for this. I've got work to do," he insisted, trying to push away again.

"You don't have time for what?" she demanded. "To talk? To act like a human being? You don't have time to speak to me?"

He looked down at her. "Maggie, let me go."

Maggie quietly released the hold on his arm and watched as he moved past her toward the tunnel. She wasn't angry any longer—she was scared. Maybe she didn't know everything there was to know about Kyle Gentry, but she knew he wasn't a purposely callous man.

"What did I do, Kyle?"

"What?" He looked up absently, turning back to her. The expression on her face had his shoulders slumping in defeat. The wooden slats fell noisily to the floor. "Maggie, you didn't do anything."

"I must have done something to make you so angry. Just tell me and I'll apologize." She breathed out a little humorless laugh. "What was it? Did I talk in my sleep? Snore? What?"

"Maggie," he whispered helplessly.

There was a moment of hesitation, where all they could do was stand and stare at each other through the gloom. Then, as though in response to the same unspoken command, they came together.

"Oh, Maggie," Kyle whispered again, his arms moving around her and pulling her tightly to him. Her cap became dislodged and her hair tumbled down her shoulders and he buried his face in its sweet mass. "Maggie, I'm sorry."

"Kyle, I was so scared," she cried, bringing her arms up and clutching him around the neck. "I thought I'd done something to make you hate me."

It wasn't a sensual embrace—the components were not there for either of them. They were merely two people—two friends—who relied on each other and who were reaching out in their time of need.

"I'm a jerk," Kyle said finally, pulling back to look down into her face. "It's not you. It has nothing to do with you."

Maggie saw it then—in his eyes, at his brow and in the thin line of his mouth. Fear. How could she have been so unaware? Why hadn't she seen it before? Had she thought he was immune to such feelings? Did being afraid fall into her exclusive domain?

It seemed ridiculous now that it had never occurred to her he would be struggling with his own fears, his own nightmares. He'd always been so strong, so capable. She'd come to rely on him to be the solid one, the one she depended on, the one to pull them through. She had looked to him for support, but who had been there to support him? He'd been thoughtful and caring and he'd been sensitive to her needs. How could she have been so blind to the need in him?

"I should have realized," she whispered. "Kyle, I should have known."

He turned his face away, some archaic portion of his male psyche still uncomfortable with her seeing him as anything but strong and capable. "I got to thinking about Conner this morning, about what would happen to him if I...if we..." His voice trailed off and he glanced at the tunnel. "It just might be our only hope now and I don't know if I can do it. I can feel my strength slipping, Maggie. I can feel myself getting weaker." He turned and looked down at her. "I've never felt weak before, Maggie. All my life I've been strong. I could throw a pass or run a play. I had it. I had the strength and the speed. I had it when I needed it. Now all I feel is it slipping away."

He pulled out of her arms and turned away. Maggie felt so helpless, so powerless. How did she comfort this strong, capable man? How did she give him back the strength he'd given her over the past few days? If he was out of hope, she would have gladly lent him hers, but the cold night and the miserable morning had rendered her faith to little more than a glimmer. Still, she would happily relinquish to him any reserves she had left.

"We're going to make it, Kyle," she told him firmly. "One way or another, we're getting out of here."

"I want to believe that, Maggie," he said, staring into the narrow icy burrow they'd worked so long and so hard on. "I want to see my son again."

She walked to his side, and followed his gaze to the tunnel. "Come on," she said, swinging the back of her hand out and giving him a swat in the rib cage. "Let's dig this sucker and climb out. I'm sick of this place."

Kyle actually felt himself smile. He'd worked through the morning in a kind of despondent, unfeeling sort of state. But now he felt almost alive again. It was hard to ignore the bleak conditions and his aching muscles. But he did the best he could. Because despite his cold hands and his and Maggie's dismal chances for success, he agreed with her. He was sick of this place, too. He was sick of the smelly mattress and the hunger pangs and the endless cold. He'd started the tunnel with little more than hope to restore their sagging spirits. But now he was getting mad.

The anger felt good. It fueled his resolve and tempered the fear. Taking a deep, frigid breath into his lungs, he bent and retrieved the slats of wood he'd dropped. After working for a moment, he'd fashioned them into a crude sort of shovel, and he walked into the tunnel and tested it out with a few fierce swipes at the snow. It was rough and it was crude, but it worked a lot better than the coffeepot.

Kyle then helped Maggie to salvage enough of what remained of the box to enable her to continue to push the snow out from the tunnel to the growing pile inside the cabin. She insisted again that he try to use her gloves, regardless of how small and badly they fit. He was only able to pull them partially up, but he had to admit they felt better than his own soaked and torn ones. So with their new tools and renewed determination, they started back to work.

The morning soon gave way to afternoon and the afternoon seemed to stretch on forever. Maggie told herself not think about the cold, or her cramping muscles, or the long hours she spent pulling. She was determined to remain optimistic, believing each allotment of snow that she shoved out of the tunnel, dragged across the cabin floor and added to the monstrous pile that now nearly filled the entire end of their small cabin brought them closer to the surface and to freedom.

But as the long hours of the afternoon dragged on, her resolve and determination began to ebb. The simple truth of the matter was that the bitter cold was making her miserable and the strained muscles in her back, her arms, her legs and her neck made every move a painful effort. As hard as she tried to disregard them, she was kept mournfully aware of the passage of each long hour. They marked their crossing with a growing degree of discomfort and distress.

Kyle worked steadily, with the same driven determination and silence he'd started with earlier. Neither of them spoke, as though both realized that even the small effort it took to speak would be that much less energy they would have to offer.

Strength was no longer an issue—they'd exhausted theirs long ago. They operated not on brawn but on reflex. They drew their energy from a resource that had nothing to do with conventional strength or customary might. Survival—as old and as basic an instinct as man possessed. It was the survival instinct that fueled their weary bodies, that nourished their efforts and bolstered them to press on.

Maggie shoved another ration of snow against the giant pile and slowly straightened. Pain stabbed at her back like a sharp, lethal knife. She felt dizzy and weak and there was barely any feeling left in her hands and feet. The cabin had grown even darker and she stumbled across the floor to the air shaft and looked up.

The sky above appeared murky and gray and the wind gusting down the pipe felt bitter and vicious. Daylight was fading quickly and soon they would be all but blinded by the blackness.

Maggie staggered back to the tunnel and stepped into it. They had made progress. The narrow passage stretched upward at a slant a good eight or ten feet. But blackness had begun to envelop them and Kyle was little more than a shadow in the darkness.

"Kyle, we have to stop," she called quietly, her breath coming in strained, heavy gasps. "It's too dark. Come inside and rest," she murmured wearily. "Come inside."

Without waiting for a response, she turned and stumbled back into the cabin. Reaching the mattress, she carefully lowered herself and collapsed upon it.

"Are the candles there, beside you?" Kyle asked, weaving through the darkness.

"Candle. Just one," Maggie corrected, reaching a hand to the floor alongside the mattress, feeling about blindly until she located it. She handed it to Kyle, who pulled the lighter from his pocket.

"I can't," he said after several failed attempts to light the wick. "Here, you hold it. My hands are too numb."

Maggie sat up, taking the candle from him and holding it until the small flame took. Kyle returned the lighter to his pocket and joined her on the mattress.

"I'm freezing." She shuddered through chattering teeth. She felt exhausted and terribly weak, but she chose to keep that to herself. Cutting through that snow had been arduous work, he no doubt felt a lot worse than she.

"I know," he mumbled, pulling her gloves from his hands. Rubbing his cold palms together, he blew a warm breath on them. "Me, too. It's going to be a cold night."

"We made progress today," she said optimistically, not wanting to think about the night ahead.

"That we did," he agreed, nodding and giving her a tired smile. He suspected, however, that despite their immense effort, they'd tunneled little better than halfway to the surface. There was still another day of digging left, maybe two, and he wasn't sure he had another day like today left in him. They were exhausted and their tired bodies were in dire need of warmth, rest and nourishment.

Maggie shivered again, shuddering loudly. "What I'd give for a blazing fire right now. Gosh, if there was just something in this place to burn," she lamented— not for the first time. She turned and looked at him, her teeth chattering loudly. "Are you sure there isn't something we could use to burn?"

He thought for a moment, considering how wonderful the warmth of a fire would feel. "The mattress, maybe, or the sleeping bag, but then where'd we be? Not to mention we'd also risk burning the whole place down."

"I'm almost tempted," she muttered, trying to control the shaking. She looked at the small flame of the candle she held. "This isn't going to last much longer."

"No," Kyle said, following her gaze.

They both watched the meek flame dance in the darkness, and tried not to think what the dark night would be like without its faint light. The flame had brought light and as long as there had been light there had been hope. Neither of them wanted to think what the darkness would mean.

"Does your shoulder hurt?" Maggie asked, taking a deep breath and breaking the somber mood.

"My whole body hurts," Kyle groaned, carefully stretching out his stiff arms and neck. "I think it's going to need a complete overhaul."

"I know what you mean," Maggie agreed, rubbing at the particularly sensitive spots on her neck and shoulders. "I always hated that phrase people use about muscles hurting in places they didn't know they had, but I think I understand it now." Setting the candle down, she lay back on the mattress, hugging herself. "If we ever get out of here, I'm heading for one of those plush spas. You know—hot mineral baths, facials, body wraps, foot rubs. Hmm..." She closed her eyes and smiled. "I'm never going to complain about the heat again. And—" She opened her eyes and pointed a determined finger up at him. "I'm never going on a diet."

Kyle stretched out beside her and they lay in the quiet stillness for a long while. They were exhausted, their bodies spent, but neither was ready for sleep.

Maggie let her mind drift, thinking about Kyle and what had happened this morning. She'd seen the look on his face, the shine of tears in his eyes at the thought of not seeing his son again. He was no monster, no abusive father. What Cindy had told her about Kyle's relationship with his son had simply not been true, and she couldn't help wonder what else that Cindy had said had been a lie.

"Kyle," she said quietly, staring up at the dark rafters.

"Yes?"

"Why did you do it?"

He turned his head and looked at her quizzically. "Do what?"

"The settlement. Why did you suddenly drop your opposition?"

Kyle's expression stiffened. "Why do you want to know?"

Under normal conditions Maggie would never have attempted to discuss such matters with her client's ex-husband without proper procedures, but conditions were far from normal, and Kyle had stopped being merely Cindy's "ex" a long time ago. He was the man who had saved her life, who had given her hope, and she owed him the truth—even if they never made it out of this icy tomb alive. "It's not a very good deal."

"It's legal, isn't it?"

"Well, yes."

"It's what Cindy wants, isn't it?"

"Yes, of course."

"Then what's the problem?"

Maggie thought about that. What was the problem? She studied him carefully—the guarded expression, the angry eyes. It was obvious he didn't like discussing this with her, and normally it wasn't like her to press the issue. Still, she couldn't shake the feeling she was playing a part in something that wasn't right. "There's no problem. It's just..."

"Just?"

"It's just," she hedged. "I don't feel comfortable about it."

"Oh?" he murmured, thinking how unimportant courtrooms and ex-wives and alimony payments all seemed right now.

Maggie glanced up at the rough wooden beams, clenching her hands into tight fists. "Cindy has told me...well, she had told me a lot of things about you, and..." She turned her head and looked at him again. "You're not at all like what she said you were."

"I'm not? And how did my loving little ex-wife describe me?" Kyle asked. There was an acid edge to his voice Maggie hadn't heard before. "No, don't bother. I can guess."

"She—well, what she said exactly doesn't really matter," Maggie replied. She took a breath. It wasn't like her to stumble over her words this way. Suddenly it was important for her to know the truth about this man. Was he the cruel, abusive husband his ex-wife had described? Or was he the brave, generous man she'd come to know these past desperate days? Maggie wanted to ask him outright. But something in his eyes warned that she was treading on dangerous ground. Still, she ignored that warning.

"What I mean to say is, I hate to see you taken advantage of," Maggie began, rising up on an elbow. "You could do a lot better. And you don't seem to be at all the way she claimed. At least, from what I know of you now," she added gently.

Kyle looked up into her soft brown eyes and felt emotion swell in his throat. He could imagine the stories Cindy had told about him. But somehow, through all that mess, Maggie had managed to see through the lies and misconceptions. Now she was asking for confirmation that what she'd learned about him here, in this cabin, was the truth. He wanted to tell her... everything. But he knew he couldn't. He couldn't take that risk, even as her eyes pleaded with him for reassurance that her instincts about him were right.

With a sigh, he rolled over on his back and stared into the dark shadows. "Maybe I got what I deserved," he said quietly. "You don't know me all that well, do you? And I don't really know you."

"I guess not," Maggie agreed. Case closed, she thought.

They lay side by side in silence for what seemed to Maggie to be the longest time. She felt suddenly self-conscious at their closeness. Then, another chill had her quaking and she wrapped her arms tightly around herself. She rubbed her hands up and down quickly along her upper arms in an effort to warm herself, but when one hand brushed along her pocket, she stopped. Feeling something inside, she reached in and pulled out the half granola bar she'd stuck in there the night before.

"Hey! Look!" She scrambled to sit up and showed him the bar. "Look what I found." She snapped what remained of the bar in half again and held it out to him. "I forgot all about this."

Kyle looked down at the small portion of granola bar and immediately felt himself begin to salivate. "Where did that come from?"

"Last night," she said, taking another small bite. She still held the half she'd broken off for him and she shook it at him impatiently. "Here, take it."

"But it's yours."

She stopped a moment and looked at him. "That's right. And I want you to have half."

He looked down at the granola bar and then back to Maggie. "Are you sure?"

"Kyle." She reached over and placed the end of the granola bar between his lips.

The bar gave them little more than a couple of bites each, but it tasted sweet and hearty and wonderful. Kyle brought out the last of the candy mints and they finished those off, too. The little bit of nourishment lifted both their spirits; their famished bodies gloried in the sweet taste of the granola and the cool refreshment of the mint.

Kyle lay back on the mattress and Maggie lay down beside him. They were exhausted, their bodies pushed beyond the limits of reason and endurance. The night loomed before them, dark and uncertain, but for the moment a quiet contentment seemed to engulf them.

At first Kyle thought the trembling beneath him was just him shivering or Maggie beside him. He was too exhausted to be concerned. But when he heard the moaning above them, he came to full alert.

"Kyle?" Maggie said, reaching for him. "Kyle, what is that? What's happening?"

He reached an arm around her and pulled her close. "I don't know. I don't know."

"It's another avalanche, isn't it?" she screamed, clutching at him.

"We'll be okay," he assured her, squeezing her tight. "It'll be okay."

But it wasn't okay, and they both knew it. The shaking seemed to go on forever, sending snow and soot streaming down the air shaft and causing the beams overhead to moan and shift ominously. Then a loud commotion in the direction of the tunnel had them both jumping.

Picking up the candle, Kyle rushed to his feet and made his way across the cabin. Left alone on the mattress without his comforting arms to protect her, Maggie curled into a ball and hugged her knees to her chest. She was terrified and she strained to watch him through the blackness.

"What is it?" she asked when he peered through the opening doorway. It was something awful. The look on Kyle's face was something she knew she would never forget.

"The tunnel," he told her, his voice flat. "It's collapsed."

Chapter Seven

In reality, the entire tunnel hadn't caved in, but the destruction was considerable. Enough to make the thought of clearing it once again seem almost inconceivable.

Maggie scrambled up from the mattress, looking over Kyle's shoulder at the havoc. A wave of nausea gripped her empty stomach and emotion welled up. Her mind reeled and the breath stalled in her lungs.

All that time, she thought dizzily. All those long, difficult hours spent laboring, the backbreaking digging and sickening cold, all the energy they'd expended burrowing that passage. Each precious inch represented a tremendous personal cost. Only now it was gone, all gone, destroyed and useless. She could hardly stand to look—the devastated remains were the saddest, most pitiful thing she thought she'd ever seen in her life.

"Oh, no," she said, almost in a daze. The despair and disappointment were overwhelming. "No. Oh, no. Oh, Kyle."

Kyle didn't know what to feel. Rage burned inside him, consuming and destroying what precious resources he had left. He wanted to strike out, to smash and shatter, to destroy and deface, and yet a deep and profound melancholy rendered him immobile. Hope had been such a fragile thread, such a delicate strand, but they had clung to it so fiercely. They'd bolstered each other and nurtured each other and sustained a spirit of hope, even in the face of insurmountable odds.

But this—this was like death. This was like a gun to the head, an arrow through the heart, a fall from a cliff, only it hurt much, much more. This had not only destroyed hope, it had sealed fates.

Only one sound penetrated Kyle's haze of anger and despair, and that was the sound of Maggie's soft cries. The sorrow in those cries gave voice to his own silent anguish and agony. He turned and in one swift motion swept her up in his arms.

What did he say to her? How was he to comfort her? Tell her not to cry, to take heart and have hope? In the light of what had happened, those banal phrases would be like lies on his tongue rather than inspirations. Don't cry, take heart, have hope? How could he ask her to do any of those things? He wanted to cry out himself; his own heart lay bleeding and his hopes had all but been dashed. There were no words, so he merely lowered his head, burying his face in her satiny mane of hair, and whispered her name.

"Maggie. Maggie."

"Oh, look at it," she said with a sob, pulling back and looking up into his sad, desolate eyes. They had lost something so precious and her heart broke. The tunnel had been something they had created together—their project, their dream...their fading hope. It had meant their very life. But now all their hard work had gone for nothing. "Our tunnel, Kyle. Look what's happened to our tunnel."

They stood for a long time in the open doorframe, clinging to each other and grieving the loss. But eventually Kyle pulled away and slowly led Maggie back to the mattress. Losing the tunnel had been devastating, but the toll on their spirits had been nothing short of catastrophic.

Maggie was exhausted, the bone-weary fatigue reaching to the very depths of her soul. The night spanned before them, long and solemn like a cold and somber procession. Resignation left her drained in a way no physical demands ever could.

"We'd better get things ready for the night," Kyle said quietly, handing her the small bit of burning candle that remained.

There'd been no need to talk about it, no necessity to explain. They both seemed to understand the ante had been upped and the stakes had risen. With all the snow from the tunnel piled nearby and the frigid winds gusting down the stovepipe, temperatures had plummeted inside the cabin. Their debilitated, work-weary bodies wouldn't be able to maintain body temperature for long. Even if they survived this night, chances weren't good they would survive the next.

Kyle moved back across the cabin and leaned the door carefully back against its open frame. It would shield them a little from the bitterness emanating from the icy tunnel. Unfortunately, there was nothing to protect them from the mountain of snow their excavating had created and that now covered nearly one entire end of the small cabin.

After checking the stovepipe to make sure that nothing had become lodged inside it during the last slide, he'd started back to the mattress, when suddenly everything went black.

"Maggie?"

"The candle," she said grimly. She had sat on the mattress and watched the last of the candle flicker and die, feeling more helpless than she had in her entire life.

Kyle reached for his lighter and let it light his way back to the mattress. "This thing doesn't have long left, either," he said, flipping the small flame off when he reached the mattress. He searched around in the darkness, finding her hand. Pulling her to her feet, he felt her body trembling. "You okay?"

"I—I'm so cold, Kyle," she said in a quivering voice. She was so drained she was surprised she felt anything, but the cold had become ever present. She couldn't control the shaking and she'd seemed to have lost the will to try.

Kyle hesitated for a moment. It was all so hopeless, so futile. What little food they'd had was now gone, the candles had been burned and even their hard-fought efforts in the tunnel had been for naught. And yet something inside him wouldn't let go, something refused to give up. He almost wished he could turn his mind off, just lie down and let what would happen happen. It would make it so much easier and there'd be no more struggling, no more worry, no more fear.

But survival instincts were strong—too strong for him ever to be content to just sit back and accept what came without a fight. So, despite the desperate conditions and cruel twists of fate, despite the lost hope and dire circumstances, despite momentous odds and dismal chances, his spirit endured and his mind struggled to find a way to carry on.

"Maggie," he said, feeling her body quake from the cold. "It's going to be rough tonight. We're going to have to do everything we can to preserve as much of our body heat as possible." He paused for a moment. "If we strip down, take off everything except our underwear we'll trap as much of our body heat as we can in the sleeping bag."

Maggie didn't even flinch. Somewhere along the line she'd come to trust Kyle Gentry. She understood he wasn't suggesting they toss off their clothes and hop into the sack together for one last fling before the pearly gates swallowed them up. To be indignant and insulted would have been ludicrous. They were down to the wire and their lives were at stake.

As weary and defeated as she was, she couldn't help feeling afraid. What lay ahead terrified her. Was it wrong to want comfort and warmth at a time like this? The thought of having Kyle's warm body beside her during this long, black night didn't offend her, it saved her.

Kyle fumbled in the darkness and found the sleeping bag. The previous nights they'd used the unzipped sleeping bag as a blanket, but tonight it would be necessary to enclose as much of it around them as possible. Working in the dark, he carefully folded the bag and zipped the ends together.

"The sleeping bag is ready," he said quietly after he'd carefully arranged it by feel on the mattress. "Hand me your parka after you've...uh, after you're inside."

Maggie was actually grateful for the absolute lack of light at that moment. Modesty wasn't exactly a concern of hers right then, but the darkness afforded a sense of privacy and made the situation less awkward and uncomfortable. Quickly she slipped out of her bulky clothing and felt her way across the mattress and into the sleeping bag.

"All set?" Kyle asked, listening intently in the darkness.

"Yes," Maggie mumbled, her teeth chattering so violently he could hear them.

Kyle hastily undressed and slipped into the sleeping bag beside her. He carefully packed their parkas on top of the bag for added warmth, then reached down and pulled the dusty plastic tarp up around them.

There was a period of extreme clumsiness once Kyle lay back. The narrow sleeping bag made quarters exceedingly close and avoiding body contact was all but impossible. Still, they both felt compelled to try. Kyle grappled with what to do with his hands, hoping not to touch or feel anything, while Maggie lay rigid as a board, afraid even to breathe.

"Maybe if I did this..." Kyle suggested, shifting his weight just a little and cautiously moving his right arm over and beneath her head. "And maybe if you just..." At Kyle's subtle urging Maggie scooted to her side and edged closer to him. "Are you comfortable?"

"Fine," Maggie whispered, but she couldn't help but feel embarrassed. With his arm around her and her head resting on his shoulder, their position was unabashedly intimate. She tried not to think about the fact that her breasts were pressed against his chest or that her abdomen was being crushed by his hip.

Kyle had thought his mind too exhausted and his body too frozen for any sensation or reaction to penetrate, but the soft, delicate feel of Maggie's body beside him had his mind coming alive with images and perceptions. She felt so deliciously supple, so absolutely female, he began to realize that as long as there was a breath of life left in his body, he would find the beauty of a woman impossible to ignore.

But she was terribly uncomfortable. He could tell in the rigid way she held herself and the quiet catches of breath he heard coming from her throat. If there had been something he could have done to alleviate her discomfort, he would have wasted no time in doing it, but it seemed there was very little he could do. Even the slightest movement created a friction of skin to skin. He dared not move; he scarcely dared to breathe.

Gradually, degree by careful degree, Maggie began to feel a fragile warmth cut through the coldness. Wherever their bodies touched—and there seemed to her no area where their bodies didn't touch—a soothing warmth began to spread around them. The warmth was wonderfully comforting, and she felt her taut muscles begin to loosen and relax.

Despite her awkwardness and embarrassment, the feel of Kyle's strong, masculine form beside her made it difficult for her to think about anything else. As the warmth relaxed her, she closed her eyes and marveled at the strength and the stamina in his hard, lean frame. How many times since they'd been trapped had she witnessed that incredible strength and stamina of his? Propelling that stovepipe up from the roof of the cabin and through to the surface had required an enormous effort, and the work he'd done on the tunnel had been nothing short of inspirational. And even after days of too little nourishment and unreasonable demands, Maggie sensed power radiating from him just as surely as she felt the warmth begin to pervade her frozen limbs.

But it wasn't just his physical strength she thought about as she lay in the darkness beside him. She thought back to a day over a year ago, when she'd sat in a courtroom and met a man she knew to be cruel and heartless. Kyle Gentry. He was the man Cindy had told her about, the man who had cheated on his wife, who had neglected his son, and the man she neither liked nor respected. It was this man she'd run into in the lobby of the Winter Haven Lodge just a few days ago.

She thought about the man who held her now. He was the man who had shared his strength, his provisions and his warmth with her. Kyle Gentry. Even his name echoing through her brain had a different ring to it. It was as though she were thinking of two different people from two different lifetimes. She hadn't liked the man she'd met in that courtroom a year ago, the man who had cheated and lied. But the man who had saved her life and with whom she now faced a dark night and uncertain future, that man had captured her thoughts and filled her heart with emotion.

So much had changed, she thought as she felt herself giving in to the warmth and the weariness. That old Kyle didn't seem to exist any longer. But, then, neither did the old Maggie. It had been only a few days since the avalanche and yet she was having trouble remembering what life had been like before. All those things that had once seemed so important—cases and clients, schedules and calendars, contingencies and billable hours—now all seemed so trifling and unimportant. Suddenly small points had risen to monumental proportions. Had she really walked in the sun and forgotten to notice its warmth? Had she really sat down to a hasty lunch at her desk and forgotten to notice how it tasted?

So much had changed, and it made her view everything differently now.

She looked back on her life. She saw clearly all the character flaws and inhibitions that had plagued her, all the blessings and advantages she'd too often overlooked. She'd spent so many years bitter about a father who had walked away and yet she couldn't remember ever having told her mother how proud of her she was. She'd worked long and hard to get ahead, to become successful and independent, and yet she'd never allowed herself the time to reap the benefits of her hard work. She'd been so careful to protect herself—had she ever truly opened her heart to someone else?

She'd do things so differently now. She'd let go of all those old hurts and all that anger. She wouldn't let the past slow her down, wouldn't let anything stand in the way of enjoying life. And she wouldn't allow a sad and bitter wife to take advantage of a generous, courageous man.

Kyle waited, listening as the sound of Maggie's breathing became deep and even and her muscles loosened and grew heavy with sleep. He drew in a deep breath, gradually allowing his own tired body to relax. The fragile warmth that had begun to blanket them felt glorious, but he hadn't actually noticed it until now. He'd been too angry, too distracted by the rage that twisted inside of him.

It wasn't fair—any of it. At that moment, he was probably closer to death than he'd ever been in his life and yet lying in the darkness with Maggie in his arms, he couldn't remember ever having felt more alive. His tired, exhausted body was virtually bursting with sensory perceptions.

It wasn't right to feel the things he did, to be thinking about what he was, but it wasn't as though he'd planned it this way. He hadn't suggested they strip down in order for him to get a cheap thrill. His intentions had been strictly honorable. He'd only been thinking in terms of surviving the frigid night. But even the best of intentions didn't stop him from reacting to Maggie's closeness. It hardly seemed right to take pleasure in holding her nearly naked body in his arms when their situation was so desperate. And yet that's just what holding Maggie was—a pleasure.

He closed his eyes to a surge of warmth and awareness. He felt the swell of her breasts rise against his chest with every breath that she took; he could pick out and recognize each delicate rib along her slender torso and his leg nestled against the taut, smooth skin of her inner thigh. Desires stormed to life and his body couldn't help but respond. He might be close to the end, but he wasn't dead yet.

Even his total exhaustion wasn't enough to squelch the ache of longing that flowed through his weary bones. It radiated like the heat sweeping through their small sleeping bag. His world had been cold and empty for so long, but she'd burst into it like a blast of sun through a cloud-strewn sky.

He'd lived in the darkness too long. He wanted nothing more than to turn to her, to slide his tired body between those silky thighs and sink into her warm softness, deep and full. He wanted to lose himself within her, to taste and touch and feel all of her. He wanted to ravage her lips, to hear the sounds of her pleasure in his ears and to hold her to him until there was nothing else—no cold, no emptiness, no dark night.

How could he explain what he was feeling? It made no sense. He was on the very edge of the precipice, looking over the rim at an uncertain future, a terrifying fate, and yet all he could think about was the woman lying beside him. She was in his heart and in his head and his body quaked at the feel of her in his arms.

He'd thought his ability to care for a woman had been lost forever. Caring took trust, and after what had happened with Cindy he'd sworn he'd never trust another woman again, let alone the lady lawyer who had treated him as though he were the worst kind of criminal. What his ex-wife had taken from his bank accounts was nothing compared with what he'd really had to pay. But Maggie had come into his life and soothed away all those old injuries. The scars from Cindy's old wounds seemed unimportant now. Now there was Maggie.

But it was too late. Time had run out. Another surge of anger ravaged him. It wasn't fair. He would never know the joy of her, would never taste the magic of her lips or know the warmth of all her dark, mysterious places.

He closed his eyes and felt the cloak of drowsiness descending just like the warmth that protected him. He didn't like needing things. He'd needed football—once—and he needed Conner—always. But right now, with desire gnawing at his groin and his soul cold and empty, he desperately needed Maggie Danner.

Maggie felt the sun caressing her, warm and luxurious. The tormenting hunger pangs were gone and with them that awful cold. She wasn't even afraid anymore, but in the warmth of the sun, she had trouble remembering just what it was that had frightened her so much. She smiled as she drifted high, floating weightless above the ground.

Snow was all around, as far as she could see, covering everything in a veil of white—the gentle slopes, the towering pines and the distant mountains. It all looked so beautiful, so fresh and clean. The air was crisp and she could see her breath in billowy white puffs. Yet she felt no cold. She was warm and safe and not afraid. She could hear the wind through the trees whispering her name. *Maggie. Maggie.*

There was a hand along her cheek and the wind became a whisper in her ear. *Maggie. Maggie.*

It was him. Kyle. He was with her. Kyle. It was Kyle who made her warm, Kyle who made her safe. She wasn't afraid because Kyle was with her.

Kyle. Kyle. Everywhere and ever present. He was whispering her name and it was a pleading, urgent sort of appeal. He was pressing a gentle kiss along her neck and against her lips. She wanted him—and in this special place, in this special dream, he wanted her, too. Kyle.

"Kyle."

The sound of her own voice surprised her and she found herself catapulted a hundred and eighty degrees back toward wakefulness. No. She shook her head, squeezing her lids tight. She didn't want to go; she didn't want the dream to end. It was filled with warmth and serenity and...Kyle. Kyle. She wanted to stay with Kyle. She wanted him to keep calling to her, to keep kissing her.

Her eyelids flickered, but she refused to allow them to open, refused to grant access to what she knew to be inevitable. She didn't want to wake up. If she kept her eyes tightly closed, maybe the nightmare would just go away, maybe she could find Kyle and the dream again.

But consciousness had already gained a toehold, and without wanting or meaning to, she'd already begun the long journey back. Somewhere in her mind it had registered that there had been a change, that the darkness was not so dark any longer and that her tired body was no longer so weary.

Morning. She had survived the cold, bitter night. But survived for what purpose? Life in a barren, frozen cabin buried beneath foot after foot of snow had become more of a waking kind of death. She wasn't ready for a world with shape and form just yet, a world where there was only ice and cold and a dismal, dreary outlook. She wanted the dream back, in which Kyle had held her and kissed her and whispered her name. She wanted back into the dream that had made her feel more alive than life made her feel.

But the seeds had been sown. Like grains of sand pouring through her fingers, the dream slipped away. She held on to what precious remnants she could—a whisper here, a caress there. Cherished mementos of that warm, peaceful place. She could hear his voice in her head, whispering her name over and over again.

"Maggie. Maggie."

Maggie's eyelids fluttered open. The whisper—it had come from her dream. Only…she was awake now.

"Maggie."

Awareness came to her in one blinding flash of sight and sound. The whisper had been no dream and neither was the man in her arms. Both were very real.

"Maggie," Kyle whispered again, his lips brushing against her neck. "Maggie, we're alive. We're alive, Maggie."

Maggie closed her eyes to the rush of emotions rioting through her. It was obvious that he was still asleep, that the brush of his lips along her neck was nothing more than a reflex, like the kiss he'd placed along her neck on that first morning.

Then the brush of his lips became an outright kiss and his hand slid up along the outside of her thigh to rest at the narrow indentation of her waist. Maggie's breath caught in her throat and she felt herself go weak all over with longing. It was so embarrassing. She had no business feeling like this. He was still asleep. He didn't even know what he was doing. It had to stop; she had to wake him up.

"Kyle?" she said hesitantly, her hand reaching out to touch him on the shoulder.

"Oh, Maggie," he murmured against her neck. His hand slid up and around her back. "Maggie, I want you."

Chapter Eight

Understanding had come about slowly. So slowly, in fact, that responses had been long in coming. First there had only been a sense of something, then an impression, before realization set in, but once it did, reactions came in a rush.

They were alive. Kyle opened his eyes, finding Maggie nestled beside him. Feeling her soft, warm body next to his had him stirring, awakening. For the moment it didn't matter what lay ahead, what dreary sentence fate had handed down or how unfair it all was. They had survived. The long frigid night was over. Once again they had cheated death. Once again they had obliterated the line between time and eternity.

"Maggie," he whispered, burying his face deep in the fragrant juncture of her neck and shoulder. She smelled warm and rich—like woman and spirit and life. "Maggie."

She stirred, a slow smile dallying the edges of her mouth. When she moved, her breasts moved against his chest. That small movement created a delicious friction and Kyle felt his body roar to life.

"Maggie," he whispered again, against her neck. "Maggie, we're alive."

His hands became restless, longing to examine and explore. Her delicate body flowed with life, warm and potent, and it spilled into his. He kissed her neck—once, twice—tasting the rich, savory flavor of her skin. His tongue made a cool, wet path to her ear and he heard a groan escape her lips.

The time for caution had long since passed and the limit on lengthy decisions and possible regrets had expired. Last night he had wanted her. His tired body had ached for her warmth and his empty soul had cried out for solace from hers. He'd held her through the long night, never knowing if the morning would ever come. But morning had come, and with it a new dawn. The fates had smiled down upon them and allowed them another sunrise. And with the new day, a small window of destiny had opened to them. Their moment had come and there was no turning back.

He moved his hard body against hers and she responded—instinctively, uninhibitedly. Their bodies migrated toward each other as though aeons of evolution had created them for that purpose alone, as though destiny had demanded that they should.

Kyle's body surged with need. He could think of nothing but being inside of her, of finding that special part of her and burying himself deep within her warmth. Making love to Maggie meant more than pleasure and satisfaction. To love her would be like being born again—mind, body, heart and soul. Somewhere through the nightmare of cold and ice, somewhere through the fear and the terror and the brutal night, he had found her—Maggie. Maggie.

And now that he'd found her, he never wanted to let her go. Living had become a glorious inauguration—no sweeter victory than that of life over death. He wanted her as he'd never wanted another woman—wholly, completely, eternally. In another time, another place, if there had been no avalanche, no gnawing hunger, no killing cold, things could have been so different. There would have been time to take things slow, time to stake claims and declare good intentions, time to plan futures and build on dreams and time for a lifetime together.

But time had run out. There would be no beginning for them, only an end. There would be no lifetime together, no plans, no dreams. Forever had come and it was now.

Kyle felt the gentle lift of her breasts against him as the rhythm of her breathing quickened and increased. Slowly, one careful degree after another, she withdrew from sleep and responses became more determined, more confident. He felt as though he'd wanted her forever, as though he'd been waiting his whole life for just this moment. And now that she was in his arms, he would not be denied his moment in the sun—not by the frigid cold, not by the gnawing hunger, not even by death.

"Maggie," he whispered, tracing the delicate pattern of her ear with his tongue.

"Kyle," she moaned, the sound of her own voice causing her to stir even more. Her body twisted restlessly, and the tiny smile disappeared from her lips.

"Maggie, we're alive," he told her again, his hand following the silky contours of her body from her thigh to her waist. "We're alive, Maggie."

"Kyle?" she murmured. Her hand slid up to his shoulder.

He could feel her body begin to move against his, and it was driving him crazy. Life flowed like liquid fire through his veins, stoked with every touch of skin to skin, man to woman.

"Oh, Maggie," he groaned, pulling back to look down into her dark, smoky eyes. "Maggie, I want you."

"Ky—" she started to say, but he wouldn't let her finish. His mouth captured hers—fully, completely, entirely.

Maggie kept telling herself that this couldn't be happening, but she felt herself surrendering to his lips. After that there had been no time for thought, no time for protest. The kiss robbed her of the ability to do anything except act and react. In the space of a moment her world had become a very simple place, existing for only one reason, one purpose. Kyle Gentry—the touch, the taste, the sight, the sound and the feel of him.

Kyle pressed her mouth open wider and his tongue plundered deep. He was cold and she filled him with warmth. She tasted so rich, so lush, and he had been hungry for so long. He felt like a starving man with a feast laid before him. His appetite had become enormous and he couldn't get enough.

He tore his mouth from her, leaving her gasping for breath, but took no heed of his own depleted lungs. He wanted more of her—now. The feel of her body naked beneath his was driving him insane. His hands found the clasp of her bra, and he pulled the confining bit of lace and satin from her. With hands and lips, he caressed her gentle beauty, burying his face in the warm, silken valley as his fingertips massaged and caressed hard, dark centers.

Maggie's head was spinning. She'd never felt like this before. She was being bombarded by one dizzying emotion after another. She was being pulled, uprooted from her comfortable world of checks and balances, reason and logic to a place where only feelings mattered, where emotions were liberated and desire reigned supreme. No longer did rudimentary concepts of right or wrong apply; there were no boundaries to stay within or restrictions holding her back. For the first time in her orderly, regimented life, it wasn't her judgment and common sense propelling her, but rather, her heart.

Kyle was doing wonderful, magical things to her with his mouth and with his hands, and her body shuddered from the onslaught. She'd never had a man want her so much, and the strength of his desire made the need in her almost unbearable. His body above her was so strong, so powerful. She wanted to capture that force, harness as much of that strength as she could.

"Kyle," she moaned, hardly recognizing the sound of her own voice. Just the feel of his name on her lips sent a fire storm moving through her—reckless, wild and out of control.

Her hands slid down his strong, solid torso, slipping beneath the elastic band of his shorts and tracing the swell of his bottom. She could feel him tremble against her, and pressed herself boldly into his warmth.

Kyle's large body shuddered and he groaned deep in his throat. Did she know what she did to him? Did she have any idea how much he wanted her? He captured her lips again, kissing her long and deep. He could think of nothing else but her. She surrounded him like the air—her scent, her taste, her very essence becoming his whole world—to bring her pleasure, his sole reason for living.

He tore his mouth from hers, his lips hungry for her neck, her breasts, her abdomen and below. She twisted and turned beneath him. Her hands on his shoulders, on his arms and in his hair incited and aroused him more, turning his blood to flame and urging him on.

His body trembled and he fought for control. But he was quickly approaching flash point, the moment when all controls would be lost. Ground zero.

He rose up above her, like an ancient warrior rising to victory. He gazed down at her, her eyes dark and rich and full of challenge.

"I love you, Maggie Danner," he said softly, lowering his lips to her. The delicious weight of his giant body bearing down upon her caused a quiver to move through her. "I love y—"

They heard it at the same instant. It could have been a whisper, a mere rustle, but it had cut through the silence like an explosion. There had been something—a sound, a noise. Something.

Their tiny, frozen world had tilted violently and skittered to a stop. Motionless, their bodies rested frozen in almost total intimacy.

"Did you hear that?" Maggie whispered, her voice barely audible.

Kyle nodded, listening. An eternity passed and then another and still they heard nothing.

Then, as suddenly as before, something shattered the stillness again and they jumped in unison.

"Was that a voice?" Maggie asked, her eyes wide and hopeful.

Kyle shook his head and vaulted to his feet, quickly starting to dress. "A dog."

Maggie watched as he pulled on his clothes, then she reached timidly out of the sleeping bag for her own. She was suddenly very uncomfortable with her nakedness and her hands trembled badly as she struggled with her clothing. That small noise—whatever it was—had penetrated their small, frozen domain and it had left her feeling strangely vulnerable and exposed.

Kyle pulled the door away from its frame, exposing the ravaged tunnel. Stepping out as far as he could, he stood and listened. Nothing—not a sound.

Turning quickly, he went back inside and walked to the air shaft, looking up it and listening. Still nothing.

He glanced across the cabin at Maggie, who now sat dressed on the mattress. His heart constricted tightly in his chest. He could still taste her on his lips and in his mouth, could almost feel what it would have been to have her warmth surrounding him. Just thinking about that had his body tensing and his blood speeding through his veins.

He glimpsed up the stovepipe one more time, cursing silently to himself. He could hear nothing, could see nothing. Maybe they'd just imagined it. Maybe there had been nothing at all.

He could have sworn, he thought darkly as he turned and started back across the cabin. He'd just had a feeling—

There was no doubt this time. They both heard it— a dog barking. They heard it once, then once again, then a few more times after that.

Maggie sprang to her feet and leapt across the cabin floor. "A dog, Kyle. It's a dog."

Kyle searched the cabin floor for what remained of the wooden box they had used the day before in the tunnel. Tearing one of the thin slats loose, he reached it up into the pipe and banged it noisily along the side.

"Here!" he shouted up the narrow shaft. "Over here, boy."

The barking grew louder and louder and before long it had become thunderous, echoing down the narrow pipe and reverberating through the cabin in a cacophony of sound. There was no way of knowing if it was one dog or an army of them, but it didn't matter. The uproar sounded wondrous after so many days of dreadful silence, and they continued to shout and call out to the outside world.

At the first sound of a human voice, tears sprang to Maggie's eyes. For an instant she and Kyle stopped their shouting and just stared at each other in wonder and disbelief. She was afraid to move, almost afraid to breathe. After so many long days of nothing, after so many bitter disappointments and such crushing blows, after all hope had been lost, could this really be happening?

Rescue.

Maggie sat back on the mattress and watched the dramatic events unfold before her. She was numb, dazed, and her exhausted, malnourished mind had difficulty absorbing all that was happening around her.

After initial contact had been made, Kyle guided rescue workers to the location of their demolished tunnel, then began to work frantically clearing the snow away as the team on the surface dug down. But Maggie couldn't move. With each armful of snow Kyle dragged out of the tunnel, she felt more and more exposed.

They were going to live; they were going to be all right. She had her life back again; she had a second chance to do all those things she'd missed and neglected before. She should have been happy; she should been jumping for joy; she should been falling down on her knees and thanking the Almighty for bringing them through this nightmare alive.

And yet she could do nothing—just sit and watch and wait.

It seemed ridiculous, she knew, but in an odd sort of way she'd grown accustomed to their small, submerged world. She'd hated the cold and the hunger and the darkness, but it had been *their* world. Their own little corner of the universe, where it was just Kyle and Maggie, where what they wanted and what they felt was all that mattered, all that would ever matter. There had been no ex-wives, no ethical restrictions, no past histories and repercussions to deal with. In their world they had talked and laughed together, they had struggled and worked for a common cause, they had held one another through the long, freezing night, bolstered each other up when spirits sagged and hope seemed all but hopeless. They had reached out to each other, and shared their warmth and their secrets, kissed each other and found . . . love.

But all that had changed now. The real world had found them, had reached through the snow and the darkness and plucked them from their frosty isolation. Kyle tore at the icy barrier that had entrapped them as though he were desperate to get out, desperate to be free. She wanted out, too. She'd prayed for the day they'd be rescued, dreamed of it, only . . . now that it had come, she found herself reluctant to let go.

Kyle didn't even feel the cold any longer. He tore into the snow with his bare hands, pushing and shoving as much out of the tunnel as he could. It was as though his weary muscles and starving body had been imbued with new energy, new strength. He wanted them out—as soon as possible.

This morning all he'd wanted was time enough to have Maggie—just once, *just once*. He'd been resigned to try and settle for what he could in what little time they'd had left. But no longer. With the arrival of rescuers, everything had changed. There was time now to think of a future, to think about hopes and dreams, and selfishly he found himself wanting more than the moment, more than one season in the sun.

It was ironic, he thought as he dug fiercely at the snow in the tunnel, but only by facing death had he finally discovered what he wanted out of life. The ball had been snapped; it was within his reach. He wanted to grab and run with it.

Their lovemaking had ended abruptly with the arrival of their rescuers—ended before it really had a chance to begin. But he had no regrets. This morning had merely been a preview of what they would share, simply the warm-up to the play-off game. Just once with Maggie would never be enough now. He wanted it all—the touchdown and the field goal—the whole enchilada. A life, a future and Maggie.

The sudden blast of light was blinding, flooding the interior of the cabin with a blanket of white like the wall of snow that had buried it. Cold, frigid air rushed in with it, stirring up dirt and debris and creating a giant gritty cloud.

Maggie came quickly to her feet, stumbling off the mattress and choking on the grimy, dusty air. She couldn't see, the piercing light having rendered her all but blind, but she didn't need to see to know that their rescuers had broken through from the surface.

"Kyle?" she called out, feeling her way blindly. Tears streamed from her stinging eyes.

"They're through, Maggie," he said, grappling about until he found her hand. Then he pulled her to him, slipped an arm around her waist and gave her a small squeeze. "It's going to be all right now, sweetheart. We're getting out of here. It's going to be all right."

They were indeed getting out, but Maggie suspected nothing was ever going to feel right again. Rescue happened for her in a blinding haze of confusion and bewilderment. Rescuers skidded down from the surface one after the other, pulling her from Kyle and strapping her with a safety vest and ropes. Somehow she was transported through the icy tunnel to the surface. She heard voices and cheers and dogs barking wildly and she was aware of others around her, but the hideous glare made it impossible for her to see much of what was happening. Finally, as she was being led to one of the rescue sleds, someone handed her a pair of dark glasses. After she slipped them on, her eyes began to adjust and the world took shape once again.

"Kyle?" she said, looking about. She turned then to the stocky man beside her, who was wearing a bright-orange vest emblazoned with the ski patrol insignia. "Where's Kyle?"

"Don't worry," he assured her, helping her onto the sled. "He's right behind you."

She glanced back just in time to see the team of rescuers pulling Kyle from the tunnel and helping him to another of the waiting sleds. He was safe and she suddenly felt as though an enormous weight had been lifted from off her shoulders.

"Hang on now," her rescuer said, fastening a harness around her. "We're going to get you down off this mountain."

Everyone was so nice to her and Maggie felt a swell of emotion. Realization might have been slow in coming, but it came in a rush now. She gazed up at the trees towering above her, at the snow, the sky. They were real—everything was real. It wasn't just a dream. She wasn't going to wake up and find herself in that dark, frozen tomb ever again. It had really happened—they'd been rescued. She was really feeling the sunshine on her face, really breathing in the fresh air, really going to live.

Tears sprang to her eyes again and she said a quiet prayer of thanks. It had been such a shock, she'd needed time to adjust. To have been pulled from the throes of passion and back into the real world had been a difficult transition to make. But now, in the sunshine, in the fresh air, she began to realize how fortunate they were.

But it wasn't until they'd reached the base of the grade that she realized just how lucky they had been. As difficult and agonizing as their ordeal in the buried cabin had been, fate had actually been more generous to them than the other guests at the resort.

The avalanche had been massive and it had been a killer. Winter Haven Lodge had all but been destroyed. Despite a desperate rescue effort, few survivors had been found. For days rescuers had pulled only victims from the frozen devastation. Brutal winter storms and the threat of other slides had hampered the progress of the rescue workers and there had been little hope of finding anyone else alive.

In one of those paradoxical twists that life sometimes likes to throw at you, it had been the threat of additional avalanches that had proved to be Maggie and Kyle's salvation. In their effort to keep avalanche conditions from developing again, members of the ski patrol had purposely begun to cause smaller slides at the higher altitudes to prevent the buildup of snow. It had been one of these smaller slides that had terrorized them and caused the tunnel they'd worked so hard on to collapse, but it had also caused the snow on the surface to fall away from their stovepipe, exposing it and drawing the attention of a passing patrol.

Because such little hope had been held that any other survivors would be found, word of Maggie and Kyle's rescue spread fast. Arriving at the makeshift camp that served as the base of rescue operations in what had once been the parking lot of the Winter Haven Lodge, Maggie and Kyle were greeted by a small army of reporters, television cameras and well-wishers.

A barrage of questions were hurled at them as they made their way to the waiting ambulances.

"How did you survive?"

"Did you have anything to eat?"

"Was it cold?"

"How did you manage to stay warm?"

"What were you doing when you became trapped?"

"How do you feel about the snow now?"

"What are you hungry for?"

There were so many question, they couldn't even attempt to answer them all.

"How do you feel about being rescued?" One female reporter managed to ask Maggie, breaking through the crowd and reaching her just as she stepped into the back of one of the emergency vehicles.

Maggie gave her a tired smile, watching as Kyle disappeared into the back of the other ambulance. "I'm thankful."

"Were you afraid when you saw the avalanche coming?"

"Very. It was very frightening."

"What did you do? What were you thinking?"

"I didn't do anything. I couldn't move," Maggie told her honestly. A paramedic was rolling up her sleeve and busily taking her blood pressure. "If it wasn't for Kyle—"

"Kyle?"

"Yes, he was the one who found the cabin," Maggie said, trying to explain. The burst of adrenaline that had gotten her through the rescue, the people and the excitement was nearly exhausted, and she was having trouble thinking straight. "I mean, he pulled me inside, out of the way."

"He saved your life, then?"

Maggie nodded. The warmth of the ambulance felt wonderful and she began to feel terribly drowsy.

"So he's your hero?"

Maggie nodded again, a tired smile curving the corners of her mouth. "My hero."

"Wow, that's great," the reporter said hurriedly. She would have only a moment before the ambulance left and she wanted to make the most of her exclusive. "So, do you think you and your husband will ever want to take a winter vacation again?"

"Oh, we're not married," Maggie blurted out without thinking.

Interest was immediately aroused. "Oh?"

"I mean, we didn't know each other—well, not very well—" Maggie stammered, flustered and embarrassed.

"So this stranger saved your life?" the reporter persisted, being shoved to one side by the ambulance driver. "How do you feel about him now?"

But Maggie didn't answer. The ambulance driver slammed the doors of the vehicle shut and they started their journey through the pass to the hospital in nearby Truckee.

How did she feel about him now? she wondered as the paramedic guided her onto the cot. She thought about the morning, about waking up in Kyle's arms, about how he had kissed her and made her feel so alive.

The paramedic, in constant radio contact with the hospital in Truckee, started an IV in her arm, but Maggie was barely aware of it. The momentous events of the day were finally catching up with her and she felt herself growing lethargic and sleepy. It was so warm inside the ambulance, and the steady drone of the engine lulled her. Her eyelids fluttered shut and her mind drifted back to the morning.

She thought about how it had felt to have Kyle's hard, strong body beside hers. They'd very nearly made love this morning. It had been only a quirky act of fate that had stopped them. She'd wanted rescue to come and she was glad now that it had. But just for a moment, she let her mind wander and she let herself imagine just what it might have been like if it had come just a few moments later.

The drowsiness became overwhelming and she gave herself over to it. Still, she couldn't help thinking, there she was, in an ambulance speeding her to safety. There were paramedics and doctors to take care of her and keep her alive. But even with this army of medical and rescue personnel, she'd actually felt safer and more alive in the peril of a cabin buried beneath twenty feet of snow with Kyle's arms around her.

Chapter Nine

Maggie opened her eyes with a start and sat up. "Kyle? Kyle?"

"Shh, shh, it's all right, everything's fine," a paramedic soothed, calming her and guiding her back down onto the cot. "It's okay. We're just pulling into the emergency."

"But where's Kyle? What's happened?" She felt so confused, so off balance. She lay back down on the cot, her heart pounding so fiercely she could feel its rumble through her entire body. Gradually, though, the fog began to lift and her memory returned. She began to remember—the dogs barking, the ski patrol, the rescue. She looked up at the paramedic who tended her so carefully. "Kyle—where is he?"

The paramedic peered through the narrow windows at the rear of the ambulance. "They're pulling up behind us right now," he told her, giving her hand a comforting pat. "Don't worry, your friend is fine. You'll be seeing him real soon now."

Maggie closed her eyes and let the flurry of activity happen around her. Gurneys, nurses, more cameras and questions—they all passed by her in a haze of action and animation. Things were happening so fast, and her tired mind and body were having a hard time catching up. She'd needed time to assimilate and absorb, but there'd been none. They'd been rescued, but it still seemed hard to believe. She watched the hustle and bustle going on about her, but felt strangely withdrawn and detached from the action, rather than an intricate part of it.

As the doctors and nurses rushed about ordering tests and completing examinations, she thought about Kyle. How was he feeling? What was he thinking about? Was he having the same difficulty digesting all of this? Did he ever think of her?

It was stupid, really, but somehow it made her feel better just knowing that somewhere in the scramble of the noisy, hectic emergency room he might be having some of the same qualms and concerns. But mostly it just made her feel better knowing he was somewhere close.

In the cabin he was the one she'd relied on, the one she'd turned to and depended on to be strong, the resourceful one, the brave one. He'd taken care of her, provided for her and made her feel safe and protected. And even though circumstances had changed and there was now an entire rescue and medical team available for assistance, she found herself still wanting to turn to him for comfort and assurance.

"Maggie?"

Hearing her name, Maggie lifted her head from the pillow. Sarah Danner looked so small and lost standing amid the chaos and confusion of the emergency room, but the love and familiarity in her faded brown eyes were something Maggie would never forget. She held out her arms, and tears welled in her eyes and splashed onto her cheeks. "Oh, Mama."

It was a warm, tearful reunion and the two women hugged and cried and held each other tight. Maggie told her mother about the avalanche, the cabin and the awful cold, while Sarah talked about long nights of worry and days of dread.

As her mother talked and quiet tears rolled down her cheeks, Maggie could see the evidence of those nights of strain and anguish in her mother's weathered face. She understood for the first time just what a toll her ordeal had been on those who loved her. She remembered the night in the cabin when she'd lain in the darkness and thought about all she regretted in her life, all the lost opportunities she'd let slip by. Realizing that if she couldn't learn from her mistakes, then there was no hope at all, Maggie decided not to let another moment pass without telling her mother what she should have said years before.

"Mama," Maggie said, grabbing a tissue and wiping at the tears on her mother's wrinkled cheek. "You worked so hard, gave us so much. I don't think I ever thanked you. I'm grateful, Mama, and I'm very proud of you."

Never had tears felt so good or second chances been more appreciated.

Later, after she'd been moved to a private room in the hospital and the doctor had given his okay, Maggie's brothers, Gary, John and Mark, her sister, Terri Lynn, her secretary, Jennifer, and a small group of friends and co-workers rushed in with love, greetings and good wishes.

The hospital had held an impromptu press conference to report on the survivors, but reporters had been kept at a distance. Remarkable to everyone, the doctor had all but given Maggie a clean bill of health, insisting, however, that she stay the night in the hospital for observation. After having gone without a sufficient intake of nutrition for so long, her body needed a slow, well-planned, well-ordered reeducation into metabolizing food again and that required careful monitoring.

It had been wonderful to see everyone and Maggie was truly touched by the love and concern of those people who meant so much to her. Life had begun to feel good again, but by the time the last of the group had left, she slumped back against the pillows of her bed, exhausted. She was amazed at how quickly the day had passed and surprised when the nurse arrived carrying her dinner tray.

In all likelihood, the steaming bowl of clear broth and jiggling plain gelatin dessert were bland and virtually tasteless, but to Maggie's neglected taste buds, they looked like rich and wonderful delights. She gazed down at the feast before her and thought she would never again take a meal for granted again.

"Hi."

The sound of Kyle's voice revived her as no meal ever could. "Hi."

The bathrobe he wore was tied loosely at the waist, but unlike the drab green hospital gown she had on, he wore only pajama bottoms beneath it. "Your family gone?"

"Yeah, a little while ago." She nodded to the tray. "Have you had your dinner yet? I'll share."

He smiled. "You go ahead. I'm not hungry."

"How can you even utter those words? I don't think I'll ever fill up."

He laughed, grimacing just a little. "Conner wanted to surprise me, brought me a cheeseburger from a fast-food restaurant. I didn't want to hurt his feelings—and it looked so good. I ended up wolfing it down."

"Oh, God, a cheeseburger," she moaned, feeling herself salivating. "Tell me what it was like—was it wonderful?"

"It was great, until my whole system decided to revolt." He rubbed a hand across his abdomen and made a face as he walked across the room and sat down on the bed. "I guess the doctor meant it when he said we had to take things slow." He surveyed the tray between them, pointing to the gelatin. "How's that?"

"Try some." She insisted, handing him a spoon, and watched as he gingerly took a bit. "Conner's here?"

"Yeah, my folks brought him with them," he said, swallowing. "We came by a little earlier to see you, but you had a mob in here."

Maggie smiled. "Family, friends, you know. It was great to see everyone." They ate quietly together for a while, but something didn't feel right. Maggie began to grow uneasy. "Will you be released tomorrow?"

"Yeah, probably." He shrugged, taking his spoon and trying some of her broth. "There's a little frost-bite on my fingers." He held up his hand to show her. "But other than that I'm okay. They tell me you're being released in the morning."

"Yes, that's right."

"Going home with your family?"

Maggie hesitated. "Uh . . . yes, I suppose."

Why had that question sounded so impersonal, as though he were just asking out of politeness? Why was he acting so differently?

But Maggie knew why. They were back in the real world again and suddenly all the old rules and standards were in place. They were no longer two people alone, two people with no one but themselves to answer to. Everything had changed. He wasn't just Kyle any longer—her friend, her savior, her . . . almost lover—and she wasn't just plain, ordinary Maggie. She was a lawyer, and he was the ex-husband of her client. There were ethical considerations and proprieties that needed to be taken into account.

She remembered what it was to lie naked in his arms. She knew what it was to hold and kiss and love him. But he wasn't holding her now. He hadn't so much as made a move to touch her since he'd walked into the room. In the darkness of their buried cabin she had only to feel and react, but in the harsh light of the hospital room she wasn't sure how to respond. The real world had come crashing down on her harder than that mountain of snow.

Kyle watched the play of emotion across her face. She was stiff and uncomfortable, nothing like the woman he had held in his arms and who had melted beneath him. He hated that awkwardness and discomfort. He didn't want her uncomfortable with him. He'd thought they'd gone beyond that—way beyond that.

He'd literally been thinking of her all day, waiting for her family and friends to leave to have some time alone with her. He wanted to hold her and kiss her, to prove to her and himself that this morning hadn't simply been a dream. But he felt foolish now.

He should have considered that she might have some regrets. It would have been obvious to a blind man that she was having some serious second thoughts now—major ones. Maybe he should be having some regrets himself, but the simple truth of the matter was that he had none, not one, zilch, zip, *nada*. He understood that involvement between them wouldn't be easy. God knows he'd had his share of complications; Cindy had made sure of that. But for a chance at a life with Maggie, he'd been willing to risk anything.

But things had happened quickly between them, maybe too quickly. And it was safe to say that the conditions of their . . . involvement had been unique. Still, that hadn't stopped him from being sure of his feelings, or of knowing what he wanted. In fact, he'd never been so sure of anything in his life. But maybe it had been unreasonable for him to think the same would be true for Maggie.

It seemed so clear to him now. She was grateful to him. He'd saved her life, and she was grateful. They'd been different people in the cabin, isolated and alone. They'd thought they were going to die. She'd needed him then and she'd relied on him to keep her safe. She'd been afraid and he had comforted her. Feelings between them had been intense and powerful and maybe it would have been easy to confuse and distort them. How could he hold her to anything that had happened between them during that dark, freezing ordeal?

But as pathetic as it sounded, he was almost desperate enough to try. He wanted her enough to do almost anything to keep her, to press almost any advantage he had, to engage any ploy that he could. He was almost desperate enough to accept her gratitude if it meant a chance to keep her in his life, almost desperate enough to accept her indebtedness.

Almost... but not quite.

What was the matter with him? Why hadn't he seen this coming? Under normal conditions a woman like Margaret Danner wouldn't give an ex-jock like him the time of day. What had happened between them had been a fluke because of the avalanche and the fact that he'd saved her life. He'd put her in an impossible position. She now had to let him down easily and find a way to let him know she just wasn't interested.

Well, he'd spare them both that ordeal. He'd back out of the picture and let her go. Spare them both a messy scene that would only be painful and embar-

rassing. He'd do it for her because he loved her, because he had no choice, because he'd rather see her
happy than hold her to a promise he knew she couldn't
keep. He'd walk away, but it wouldn't be easy. In fact,
it would be a little like dying inside.

The irony wasn't lost on him. If they'd stayed in
that cabin, it would have meant a sure death to them
both. But staying in the cabin would have meant she
would have been his. He would have held her and
loved her until life had left their frozen bodies. But
instead they'd been rescued. Their lives had been given
back to them; they'd been spared. He had a lifetime
ahead of him now, a lifetime without her. But how
empty it was to live if he couldn't have what he
wanted.

"You know," he said finally, setting the gelatin he'd
been eating back down on the tray. "I came in here
because I thought we should talk. You know, about
what happened. The cabin. You and me."

Maggie pushed the tray aside and swung her feet to
the floor. She didn't want to hear this; she didn't want
to see his face when he told her everything was a mistake. She stood on legs that were weaker and more
unsteady than when she'd toiled long and hard on the
tunnel. "Oh?"

"Well, things are liable to be kind of crazy in the
morning—you know, with all the reporters and everything. We might not have another chance... Anyway, I didn't want you to..." He closed his eyes to the
surge of raw pain. "I mean, you've nothing to
feel... uncomfortable about. We did what we had
to... in order to survive. Things were a little crazy back

there. I didn't want you to think that you... that you obligated yourself to anything."

"I see," she whispered, feeling colder and more isolated than she had under twenty feet of snow.

"I think you were wonderful—brave and strong," he went on. The pain was like an open wound, but he forced himself to finish. "I don't think I could have made it without your help."

She let out a sad, humorless laugh. "You're the one who dragged me out of the path of an avalanche, remember?"

He managed to smile. He was glad she'd turned away, glad he didn't have to face her. He couldn't have stood it then. He'd probably have fallen at her feet and made a bigger fool of himself than he had already. He kept praying that by some miracle she'd stop him, that she'd tell him to stop talking nonsense, that nothing had changed between them, that she still felt the same, that she wanted him, but that miracle never came.

"Anyway," he managed to say, his voice tight and strained. "I just wanted to say thanks and to make sure you were all right with... with everything."

"I'm fine, Kyle," Maggie whispered, staring through the small hospital window at the cold, wintry panorama of snow and darkness outside. There was too much emotion in her heart to say more. "Thank you, too."

She continued to stare out into the darkness long after she'd heard him leave. She tried to tell herself it was better this way. It made things much easier, much less complicated, but she wasn't very convincing. It hurt too much for anything good to be happening.

But she had to start pulling herself together and look on the bright side. She'd just been rescued, for heaven's sake. She had to shake this heavy feeling in her heart and start thinking about all the good things in her life, about all she had to live for.

But gazing out the window at the snow-covered mountains that surrounded the small mountain community, she saw her life stretched out before her, looking as cold and as barren as that icy terrain of white.

"He's going to pay for what he did to me. I want you to make him pay."

Reaching into her drawer, Maggie pulled out a box of tissues and slid it across the desk to the woman sitting across from her. She watched as her newest client wiped at her tearstained, mascara-smudged cheeks, and wondered how many times in the past eight years of practice she had heard different versions of this same story over and over again. An aging husband, a much younger woman, a vindictive older wife—they had almost become standard elements in so many of the divorces she handled. But even though Ellen Sullivan's story wasn't particularly unique, her pain was very real.

For the better part of the past hour, Maggie had sat quietly and listened to the attractive woman in her mid-fifties tell of having stumbled upon her husband's infidelity almost by mistake. The discovery had left the poor woman emotionally devastated.

Emotionally devastated. Maggie knew a little something about that now. It had been four weeks since she and Kyle had been pulled from an icy tomb, four weeks since all the flurry and publicity and four weeks since she'd last seen him. But all that would end in a few hours. A meeting was scheduled at Kyle's attorney's office this afternoon. All parties were to meet to formally sign the property agreement.

Maggie unclenched her fists and looked at the moisture that had formed in the palms of her hands. She was nervous already.

She had been glad to get back to work, glad to have had something to keep her occupied and her mind busy. But he'd never been far from her thoughts. He was always there—inside her head and her heart—keeping her company while her mind wandered in the courtroom, lying beside her during the long, lonely nights. She remembered everything about him—the sound of his voice, the color of his eyes, the strong, solid feel of his arms. She remembered massaging his weary muscles, remembered feeling the strength in his shoulders. Who massaged that powerful frame of his now? Who did he tease and laugh with? Who did he hold and whisper to in the night?

I love you, Maggie.

He had whispered those words to her and she heard them every night in her head. Maybe at that moment he had loved her, but he didn't love now. Maybe at that moment there had been some real feelings, something more than desperation, something more than need and response. Maybe at that moment there had been love in his heart.

"So what do you think?" Ellen Sullivan asked, looking at her red and swollen eyes in the mirror of her small compact. "Could I keep the house?"

Maggie looked up, setting her own thoughts aside and thinking about the dilemma of the woman across from her. Raymond Sullivan owned and operated a successful business and the chances of Ellen getting a big part of that business looked good. Financially, the woman wouldn't have a thing to worry about.

Yes, this was just the kind of case Maggie normally liked to sink her teeth into, the kind she specialized in. The man had devastated his wife and hurt his family and he would have to be made to pay. It was the kind of case that usually had Maggie springing into action, but there was something different about this one, something that had her holding back.

She glanced at the small rock on her desk, the rock that had once clogged the stovepipe in the cabin. She'd discovered it in the pocket of her parka on the morning she'd left the hospital.

Something had changed, all right, but not *something*. Someone. She had changed. She was different and it made the way she did her job different, too. She remembered how she'd felt when she'd first met with Cindy Gentry. Even though she'd always told herself there were two sides to every story, she'd believed everything Cindy had told her—about all the abuses, about all the other women—everything. After that first meeting, Maggie had gone after Kyle with both barrels loaded. It hadn't even occurred to her that Cindy would have been less than honest with her, that she would have stretched the truth and exaggerated the facts.

But she knew now. She knew because she knew Kyle. And the man she knew didn't even resemble the one Cindy had described to her. He wasn't abusive, he didn't neglect his son and he was too honest, too forthright ever to be unfaithful. But she'd found it out too late. He was going to have to pay for the rest of his life because of the aggressive campaign she'd waged against him and there was nothing she could do to stop it. She was bound by a code of ethics and standards that prevented her from advising him. In a few hours from now she would be forced to step back and watch him sign his life away.

But even though she couldn't help Kyle, there were other things she could do. She could choose to not make the same mistake twice. She could never again go off half-cocked, without the whole story, without looking at both sides. It was time she stopped reacting like that little girl who'd been abandoned by her father and it was time she put that old battle to rest once and for all.

"Ellen, do you love your husband?"

"Love him?" she gasped, tears springing to her eyes once again. "He cheated on me. He lied to me."

"I know that, but do you love him?"

"How could I after what he did?"

"You've lived nearly thirty years with the man. You raised three children with him. Were they all bad years?"

"Well, no, of course not," she said, dabbing at her eyes. "But he cheated—"

"He made a mistake."

Ellen Sullivan looked at Maggie, her eyes dry now. "What are you trying to say?"

Maggie got up and slowly walked around her desk. "You're hurting and you're angry—you've every right to be. But it was one night, Ellen—one mistake. Are you ready to throw away thirty years because of something that might just be one isolated incident?"

"You mean I should forgive him? I should just turn the other cheek. Pretend it didn't happen?"

"No, no, not at all. But I'm saying there's no need to rush into anything." Maggie paused, then reached down and took Ellen's hand. "I plan on being here for a long time. I'd just like you to go home and think about things for a while. Talk to your husband, Ellen, maybe look into getting some counseling. Then, if you still think you want to go ahead with this thing, I'll be here. I'll do everything I can for you."

"Y-you really think that would be best?" the older woman asked.

Maggie shrugged, helping her into her coat. "I think this is something we don't need to rush into." After a moment longer, Maggie ushered her out of the office to the secretary's desk. "Jennifer, would you see that Mrs. Sullivan gets a copy of our referral list of marriage counselors?"

After making a few recommendations on counselors, they talked a short while longer. When she turned to leave, Ellen Sullivan stopped suddenly and gave Maggie a quick, unexpected hug before rushing down the corridor toward the bank of elevators.

"Another satisfied customer?" Jennifer asked dryly.

"Isn't there something you should be typing?" Maggie teased back.

"Correct me if I'm wrong, but didn't we just talk ourselves out of a case?"

Maggie looked back down the corridor and shrugged. "Maybe. But maybe we just saved a marriage." She turned around to find Jennifer scrutinizing her. "What?"

"Nothing," the young woman said thoughtfully, shaking her head. "I just...forget it, never mind." The phone rang and she quickly answered it. "Call for you on line two."

"Thanks," Maggie said, heading back to her office.

"And don't forget you've got a two o'clock at Steve Berg's office—the Gentry settlement," Jennifer reminded her quickly.

"I won't," Maggie mumbled, feeling her stomach begin to knot. It was not going to be an easy meeting.

She walked back to her desk, reached for the phone and pressed the blinking hold button. "Hello, this is Margaret Danner."

Chapter Ten

"Hello? Is anyone on the line? Hello?"

Kyle listened to her voice, bracing himself for the sudden rush of emotion. He opened his mouth to speak, but the words stalled in his throat.

Quietly he slid the receiver back onto its cradle and cursed violently under his breath. When had he become such a coward? He'd had a reputation on the football field of never backing down, of going after the impossible. He'd never been intimidated by bulk or the threat of injury. That was probably why he'd been able to hold his own against some of the toughest players in the NFL. So why was it that one stunning lady lawyer with eyes the color of the lush, rich mink could turn him to jelly and render him to little more than a wimp?

He was exhausted. Almost as tired as the day they'd pulled him from that icy cabin beneath the snow. It had been a hellish month since the rescue. He hadn't slept, hardly felt like eating and had no interest in work. He was a wreck. He'd been grateful when all the hoopla and attention of their ordeal and rescue had finally died down, but getting back to normal hadn't been easy. In fact, he was beginning to think he'd never feel normal again.

He looked down at the telephone sitting mute and useless on his desk and cursed himself again. God, he was weak. Why hadn't he just said something? Why hadn't he just asked how she was, what she'd been doing—anything but that cowardly silence. Why had he even bothered calling?

He knew why. He knew because even if he hadn't the courage to talk, it had been enough just to hear her voice.

He was pathetic.

It seemed the only thing that kept him going these days was Conner. Cindy had been so busy with her ski weekends and shopping trips to San Francisco and L.A. that she'd been leaving the little boy with him more and more. But Kyle didn't mind. He preferred it when Conner was with him. Conner put no restrictions on him, made no demands. He was just a child who loved his daddy—no problems, no motives and no questions asked. That kind of unqualified acceptance was just what Kyle needed in his life. He hoped that once the papers were signed this afternoon and Cindy got in writing everything she'd demanded from him, she wouldn't need to use the boy to threaten or intimidate him any longer. Maybe he could finally convince her to sign permanent custody of Conner over to him. The boy had served his purpose, his usefulness was at an end.

He thought about the meeting and the chance to see Maggie again. It wasn't going to be easy. It would be difficult just being in the same room with her, trying to pretend there had been nothing between them. Was he just supposed to forget that he'd held her in his arms, that he'd touched her and kissed her and told her that he loved her?

Sitting in the small cluttered trailer that served as a makeshift construction office on the site of his latest commercial development, he wasn't sure yet just how he was going to accomplish that. How he was going to stand around like an idiot and smile politely at her, offer her his hand, make small talk, ask about business, comment on the weather? How could he do that when his arms ached to hold her, when he went to bed each night wanting her, when he knew he loved her more than he loved his own life? The past few weeks without her had been agony, but to see her and talk with her, be with her and not be able to touch her, would be nothing short of torture.

Just then the door of the trailer opened, causing Kyle to jump and sending his thoughts scattering.

"Sorry," his foreman, Skip Larsen, said. "What's got you so nervous? We're ahead of schedule, you know."

"It's nothing," he mumbled, absently shuffling the papers in front of him.

"You know those inspectors are due through here this afternoon. You'll be around for that, won't you?"

"Damn," Kyle swore, shaking his head. "I forgot. I'm sorry. Look, I've got an appointment at my lawyer's office this afternoon. I don't know how long I'll be tied up. If there's a problem tell them to give me a call."

"Lawyer, huh? Problems with your ex? Is that what's been eating at you the past several weeks?"

"Not really," he groaned, rubbing at his scratchy eyes. "Just problem problems."

"Ahh, a new woman."

"What makes you say that?"

"Hey, I recognize the signs, man. You're in a bad way. That can only mean one thing. Some woman's gotten under your skin." He walked over and patted Kyle on the shoulder. "I'm afraid you've got it bad, my friend."

The foreman grabbed his hard hat and headed back outside, leaving Kyle to mull over his words. Skip had been right. But it wasn't just a woman that had gotten under his skin. It had been *the* woman.

Maggie stepped off the elevator onto the seventeenth floor, feeling as though she'd left her stomach several stories below. Steven Berg's offices weren't nearly as large as those of Abernathy, Fox and Slone, but they made up for it in plushness. Located in one of Sacramento's newest and tallest highrises, they provided a breathtaking view of the skyline of the city through smoked-glass windows.

"Hi, I'm Margaret Danner," she said to the attractive receptionist seated behind a giant marble counter. "I have a meeting with Mr. Berg."

"Oh, right, Miss Danner, hello." The young woman
smiled. "Steve's on a conference call at the moment,
but he's expecting you. Your clients are already here.
They're waiting in the conference room. Third door
on your right."

Clients. Steve's and hers. Kyle and Cindy. Maggie's
stomach rolled squeamishly.

I can get through this, she told herself. *I'm not going to throw up. I can handle this. It's going to be all
right.* But even as she quietly repeated that litany to
herself over and over again, she felt perilously close to
losing the lone cup of coffee that inhabited her otherwise empty stomach.

She thanked the young woman and started the fate-
ful trek down the long, mauve carpeted corridor. She
dreaded this meeting, just as she'd dreaded those cold,
awful nights in the cabin. And yet, she was going to
see Kyle again. He was there, just a few feet down the
hall. She had to stop herself from running down the
lushly carpeted passageway and throwing herself into
his arms.

Halfway, she stopped to take a deep breath and give
her hair a quick shake. She slid her tongue along her
dry lips, but it didn't help much. Her mouth felt as
arid as a desert. Nervously, she ran a hand down the
length of her sleekly tailored, light-gray pin-striped
suit, wishing now that she'd worn something else,
something less severe, less businesslike.

But this *was* business, she reminded herself. This
was strictly business...even though in her heart it felt
very personal. This was just the last detail left in the
whole Gentry affair...uh, case. Signing the final pa-

pers was little more than a formality, really. After today's meeting, all actions would be concluded. She
could go back to her office, hand the folder to Jennifer and have her file it away in their archives of closed
cases. Put an end to it once and for all.

An end.

A swell of emotion rose in her throat. It was an end.
After today, there would be no reason to see Kyle
again. It would all finally be over—the divorce, the
rescue—everything. After today she would not only
close the file on the case, but on this chapter of her
life, as well. But how did she do that?

Nervously tensing and relaxing her grip on the handle of her briefcase, she started once more toward the
double doors of the conference room. At the doors she
hesitated. One stood partially open, and she heard
voices from inside.

At the sound of Kyle's voice she felt herself go weak
all over. It sounded so endearing, so familiar.

I love you, Maggie.

Desperately she blinked back the sting of tears that
had somehow sprung up in her eyes and drew another
cleansing breath into her lungs. Kyle and Cindy were
talking about Conner and Maggie was reluctant to
disturb them. She knew how important it was that the
lines of communication between parents remain open
after a divorce. Communication between Kyle and
Cindy hadn't always been good in the past. But they
were talking now and hopefully they had worked
through the rough spots—at least she hoped so for
Conner's sake. She knew how important his son was

to Kyle and knew he'd go a long way to protect his relationship with the child.

It really hadn't been her intention to eavesdrop. She'd merely wanted to allow them some privacy to discuss their mutual concerns for their son. She'd actually taken a few steps back in order to take herself out of earshot, but there was something that had her stopping and turning to the open door again.

They were talking about Conner, all right, but it had nothing to do with visitation schedules and holiday vacations.

"Look, either we do it my way or it's not getting done," Cindy was saying.

Kyle let out a frustrated sigh, running a hand through his shaggy hair. "Hasn't he been hurt enough by the divorce? He's just a little boy. He needs stability right now, not more vague promises. Why are you doing this?"

Cindy's laugh was a low, self-satisfying sound. "Oh, Kyle, darling, you know better than that. I do it because I can."

Kyle slammed his fist down hard on the dark, smoothly polished surface of the mahogany conference table. "Don't push me, Cindy, damn you. Don't push or I swear to you I'll—"

"You'll what?" Cindy demanded, cutting him off. "Cut me off? Expose me?" She laughed again. "That would be a little like tightening the noose around your own neck, wouldn't it?" She purposefully lit the end of a very long cigarette and blew a long plume of smoke in his face. "Remember, friend, you've got the most to lose here. Not me. I'm calling the shots. You wanted out so badly, you wanted a divorce—fine—I gave you one. But don't forget for a minute we're doing this my way—that was the deal. Just keep in mind, the press is still crazy about their fair-haired quarterback—especially now that he's such a hero, saving beautiful damsels in distress and all."

"That's enough, Cindy."

"Wouldn't they just love this little bombshell."

"I said that's enough," he shouted.

"Oooh, Kyle, you're frightening me," she purred sarcastically. "You're a hero now. Be careful or you might tarnish that sterling reputation of yours. And honestly, that really was rather big of you. I mean, saving my lawyer's life was really above and beyond the call. And I suppose she was just ever so grateful." She inhaled another long draw of smoke and blew it out. "Tell me, just between you and me, weren't you tempted even once during all those long, lonely nights playing the big strong hero with Margaret to tell her just a few of the dirty little details of our arrangement?"

"Leave Maggie out of this."

"Oh, it's 'Maggie' now. My, my, my, just what went on between you two down there? Just how grateful was she? Oh, she's attractive enough, I'll admit that, but after our little talks I'm afraid she thinks you're something of a bastard."

"Cindy, I'm warning you."

"But she's a smart lady. I guess our 'private arrangement' wouldn't have bothered her, anyway. She gets her considerable piece of the Kyle Gentry pie now, too, doesn't she?"

"Don't do this, Cindy," Kyle warned. "Push me and I'll tell Conner."

"Tell him what?" she sneered, crushing the cigarette out in the smoked-glass ashtray. "The truth? That his perfect Daddy isn't really his daddy, after all? I know I can't narrow it down to just one possibility, but I could point to a picture of the entire defensive end of the Blues and tell him to take his pick."

Realization hit Maggie like a wall of ice and snow. An avalanche. It all made sense now—Cindy's unreasonable demands, Kyle's willingness to sign the unfair settlement, everything. Conner wasn't Kyle's natural child.

This was the smoking gun Cindy had been using, the knife she had twisted to blackmail Kyle into doing what she wanted.

Maggie closed her eyes tight. She was furious, at herself and at Cindy. What a fool she had been. She had bought Cindy's wounded-wife routine hook, line and sinker. How could she have been so blind? She should have been able to see how Cindy had been using her. Cindy Gentry's dirty little scheme had made her dirty, as well.

Well, no more. Maybe she couldn't go back, couldn't rethink and make up for everything that had happened, but she could damn sure put a stop to things now. Taking a deep breath, she stormed through the conference-room doors and tossed her briefcase onto the table, then turned to Cindy Gentry.

"You're a real piece of work, lady, you know that? I used to think I'd do anything I had to get my client what she wanted—push the limits of the law, of ethics—anything. But by God, I won't be lied to. And I won't be a party to blackmail."

Cindy's mouth dropped open, her face was stiff and pallid. "Look, Margaret, I—"

"You call yourself a mother?" Maggie cut in, shaking her head in disgust. "You're pathetic. You don't deserve a child, and you sure as hell don't deserve this." She opened her briefcase, pulled out the settlement papers and tossed them into a nearby wastebasket. "I've got some advice for you, Cindy— and this time it's on the house. Find another lawyer. I quit." She flipped her briefcase closed. Anger had numbed all other emotions, all inhibitions. Without pausing for a breath, she turned to Kyle. "You're a good man, Kyle, a good father. Go to Conner—go to your son. Tell him the truth. He loves you. You're his father in all the ways that matter." Then she lifted her briefcase off the table and headed for the door. With her hand on the knob, she turned back for one last look. "There's more to being a father, Kyle, than bloodlines. Believe me, I know."

Kyle stared after her, his whole body glowing with warmth as though finding the sun after too many long days without it. Maggie. She'd been magnificent, commanding, dynamic, jumping to his defense with all the fiery indignation she'd had when he'd suggested she share a dirty, rotting mattress with him.

Fired up, Maggie Danner was a force to be reckoned with—and Maggie had been fired up. Cindy had been visibly shaken by the encounter. Kyle glanced at his ex-wife and almost felt sorry for her. Almost.

"This changes nothing," she said, but her voice was unsteady and he saw the fear in her eyes.

"It changes everything."

"Kyle Gentry, I warn you."

"Save it, Cindy," he said quietly, heading for the door. "The deal's off."

Maggie charged down the corridor toward the elevators, feeling as though a ten-ton weight had just been lifted from her shoulders. Looking up, she saw Steve Berg walking toward her, heading for the conference room.

"Hey, Maggie, where you going?"

"The meeting has been canceled, counselor," she said, brushing past him. "Cindy Gentry needs a new lawyer."

"But wait—" he started to say, but she left him standing in the hallway and disappeared around the corner. He'd turned to head for the conference room again, when Kyle suddenly pushed past him. "What the hell's going on around here? Kyle—wait!"

But Kyle was oblivious to everything. He rushed past Steve, chasing down the hall after Maggie like a man on a mission.

The elevator doors opened with a quiet swoosh and Maggie stepped inside the empty enclosure. She'd just reached for the lobby button, when Kyle appeared suddenly from around the corner.

"Maggie," he called out, panting and breathless from having run down the corridor. "Maggie, wait."

He stepped inside the elevator just as the doors swooshed closed behind him.

"You should have told me," she said abruptly, still angry.

"I couldn't," he replied, his eyes drinking in the sight of her like a man lost in the desert quenching his thirst from the spring of an oasis. Suddenly everything had become so clear, so obvious. He wasn't floundering as he'd been the past four weeks. One moment in a room with her and he knew what it felt like to live again. He knew exactly where he was going—exactly what he wanted. "She threatened to go back to court with a custody suit—one that challenged my rights to have anything to do with Conner."

"Oh, and signing over everything you own to her would solve everything?" She turned away in frustration and began pacing back and forth across the slate floor of the elevator. "What were you thinking?"

"I don't know," he confessed, leaning back against the paneled wall and watching her. She moved with sure, graceful motions and he remembered how she had moved beneath him with the same poise and grace. "I was scared. I believed her threats and I just couldn't take that chance. I thought if she got what she wanted—"

"What? She'd just go away?"

"No, but if I had nothing else to give her, what more could she want?"

"Damn it, Kyle, do you have any idea how naive that sounds?"

"What was I suppose to do? He's just a little boy, and he's been through so much already—the separation, the divorce. Even if Cindy didn't drag me through some brutal paternity suit, I still didn't want Conner to find out the truth. Not yet, anyway. I couldn't hurt him that way. I didn't want him to know how his mother had betrayed me with my own teammates when I'd tried to leave her." He paused, and his voice softened. "He needs me, Maggie. And I need him, too."

Maggie's first impulse was to simply reach out and put her arms around him, to do what she could to ease the pain in his eyes. She stopped herself. Her lawyer's mind worked out the options—building on some, rejecting others.

"We have to take care of first things first," she said thoughtfully, looking up at him. "You have to go to him, Kyle. You have to go to Conner, right now, right away. Tell him the truth. Get the whole thing out in the open. He doesn't need to know all the ugly details of what his mother did or why. He needs to understand that no matter what, you're still his daddy and you love him, and that will never change. That's all that's important."

Kyle could almost see the wheels turning in her mind and his heart tripped in his chest. She was amazing—cool, smart and decidedly professional. He listened intently to what she was saying, but all he could think of was pulling her into his arms, of ravaging her mouth and carefully pulling that staid, sedate business suit from her beautiful body—piece by piece. But he made no move to do that. For the time being he was content to just lean back and watch her.

"We've got to come up with something definite," she said, her mind moving to the next step as she started pacing again. "Otherwise it'll never stop. There will always be some new demand, some new condition. We'll get another settlement drafted, one that's fair to all sides. We'll present it to her, and if she balks or starts up with her old tricks again, we'll just get stubborn." The elevator stopped and she marched into the lobby. "Wait her out. See how she likes that. What do you think—" She pulled up short. "Kyle?" She looked around, confused and surprised to discover he wasn't with her. "Kyle?"

She turned back around and saw him still standing in the elevator, a wide smile beaming across his face. "What are you doing in there?" She stepped back inside and let the doors slide closed behind her as the elevator began ascending. "What are you just standing in here for?"

"We?"

"What?" She laughed a little, still confused. "What are you talking about?"

"You said *we.*"

"Did I?"

"Yes, you did."

"So?"

"Did you mean like you and me?"

"Yes."

"Us?"

"Yes, us. What is wrong with you?"

He pushed himself away from the wall and took a step toward her. "You're willing to represent me?"

"Well, no—uh—I—uh, it's not appropriate for me to represent you." She felt foolish now, and stumbled back a step. What had she been thinking about? Her role in all of this had ended. What was she doing plotting strategy and planning attacks? "But I—of course I'd be happy to make myself available for any questions you might have."

"I see," he said quietly, reaching a hand out and pushing an errant hair back away from her face.

"U-unless, of course," she stammered, taking another step backward, "you would simply prefer I back off..."

"Oh, no," he said simply, reaching around behind her. "I want you."

The elevator suddenly lurched to a stop. Maggie braced herself, then reeled around, to find Kyle's thumb on the emergency button.

"What are you doing?" she asked, looking up at him. "Why did you stop it?"

He looked down at her and smiled. "We're trapped. Stuck."

"Kyle, what are you doing?"

"And it's so cold in here," he went on, pulling the briefcase from her hand and tossing it into the corner. His hand slipped to the buttons of her suit jacket and carefully unfastened them. "I hope we don't freeze to death."

"Kyle," Maggie whispered, feeling herself grow weak. "Kyle, please."

"Hold me, Maggie," he said, slipping his hands beneath her suit jacket and sliding his arms around her waist. He drew her closer, relishing the feel of her. "Hold me and make me warm again."

"Kyle, please, don't," she protested, but her arms remained lifeless at her side. She couldn't think when he was holding her, couldn't stop herself from hoping. "Please don't do this."

"Don't do what Maggie? Don't touch you? Don't hold you? Think about it." He closed his eyes and pulled her to him tightly. "Remember how good it felt? It's been so long Maggie. I want to feel good again. I want it to be the way it was for us in the cabin."

"But we can't, Kyle." She struggled, her hands pushing against his shoulders. She couldn't handle another brief encounter, another fleeting incident. Her feelings were too strong for that, her emotions too deep. "I can't, I—"

But he wouldn't let her finish. He kissed her, sending her senses spinning and ending any protests. It no longer mattered why he was there, or for how long. He was there with her for the moment, and that was all that mattered. She'd lost all notion of time and space, unaware that her hands had somehow made their way up and were now clutching the lapels of his jacket.

"Oh, Maggie, God, Maggie," he groaned, tearing his mouth from hers and holding her close to him. "We're alive. We survived. What are we doing?" He pulled back and looked down at her. "Why are we acting as though nothing happened, as though we can go back to the way things were before? We've been given a second chance, Maggie, a chance I never thought we'd get. Don't we owe it to ourselves to be happy? Isn't it our duty to make the most of our lives? I love you, Maggie. You're what I want, what makes me happy."

"Oh, Kyle," she whispered, feeling the floor beneath her sway, even though the elevator had not budged an inch.

"Marry me, Maggie. Please marry me. I know it's fast. I know how you feel about marriage. But I love you."

"You love me?" Maggie repeated, her ears ringing with the glorious sound of those words again.

"I love you," he said again. "And if you weren't so stubborn you'd admit that you love me, too."

She looked up at him. Kyle loved her and wanted to marry her. Could it be true? Did dreams ever come this close to being real? "B-but what about Conner? What if he doesn't like me, what if—"

"Conner already knows how I feel. I told him all about you. We'll go to him together. We'll tell him the truth. You said it yourself, Maggie. We love each other. That's all that's really important."

Maggie felt like crying. He was right, of course. She did love him. But marriage—did she dare let herself take a chance?

She'd once believed marriage was something she would avoid at all costs. That words like *commitment* and *devotion* faded with the test of time, promises were made to be broken and forever meant the moment. But she'd learned many things on that mountain a month ago. She'd learned about generosity of spirit and the will to survive. She learned about what two people could do when they trusted each other and bonded in a common cause, and love could be a very strong cause.

Kyle hadn't just saved her life—he'd given her a whole new one. And even facing an icy death beneath a mountain of snow, she'd felt more alive there than she had in the empty days since the rescue.

"I feel like I'm dreaming," she whispered, "but I'm scared a little, too."

Kyle smiled at the honesty of her comment, and exhaled slowly. It wasn't until that moment that he realized just how rigidly he'd been holding himself. "Don't be scared, Maggie. I'll be right there beside you."

"This love stuff is all new to me."

"It's all new to me, too."

Slowly she let her arms travel up and encircle his neck. How had she managed to get through a whole month without holding him close like this? "Well, okay, you got a deal."

Kyle smiled, feeling almost giddy. "Say it, Maggie. Let me hear you say it. It would make me very happy," he confessed.

She smiled, realizing how saying the words would make her happy, too. "I love you."

"And?"

"And what?"

"And the marrying part."

"Oh," she said, her smile growing wider. "And I'd love to marry you. Satisfied now?"

"More than you know," he murmured, pulling her close for a long, slow kiss.

"Oh, and one more thing," she added, breathless and a little light-headed from the kiss.

"Another amendment, counselor?"

"Just one. A honeymoon someplace tropical, *please.*"

* * * * *

THANK YOU FOR SHOPPING AT THE
BOOK RACK. PLEASE COME AGAIN.

HE'S MORE THAN A MAN, HE'S ONE OF OUR

Fabulous Fathers

THE BIRDS AND THE BEES
by Liz Ireland

Bachelor Kyle Weston was going crazy—why else would he be daydreaming about marriage and children? At first he thought it was beautiful Mary Moore—and the attraction that still lingered twelve years after their brief love affair. Then Mary's daughter dropped a bombshell that shocked Kyle's socks off. Could it be young Maggie Moore was *his* child? Suddenly fatherhood was more than just a fantasy....

Join in the love—and the laughter— in Liz Ireland's *THE BIRDS AND THE BEES,* available in February.

Fall in love with our **FABULOUS FATHERS!**

Silhouette
ROMANCE™

FF294

Relive the romance. . .
Harlequin and Silhouette are proud to present

A program of collections of three complete novels by the most
requested authors with the most requested themes.

Available in February:

It was over so long ago—yet now they're calling,
"Lover, come back!"

Three complete novels in one special collection:

EYE OF THE TIGER by Diana Palmer
THE SHADOW OF TIME by Lisa Jackson
WHATEVER IT TAKES by Patricia Gardner Evans

Available wherever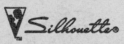

books are sold.

SREQ294

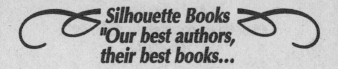

Silhouette Books
"Our best authors,
their best books...

DIANA PALMER
Soldier of Fortune in February

ELIZABETH LOWELL
Dark Fire in February

LINDA LAEL MILLER
Ragged Rainbow in March

JOAN HOHL
California Copper in March

LINDA HOWARD
An Independent Wife in April

HEATHER GRAHAM POZZESSERE
Double Entendre in April

**When it comes to passion,
we wrote the book.**

BOBQ1

**And now for
something completely different
from Silhouette....**

Unique and innovative stories that take you into the world of paranormal happenings. Look for our special "Spellbound" flash—and get ready for a truly exciting reading experience!

**In February, look for
One Unbelievable Man (SR #993)
by Pat Montana.**

Was he man or myth? Cass Kohlmann's mysterious traveling companion, Michael O'Shea, had her all confused. He'd suddenly appeared, claiming she was his destiny—determined to win her heart. But could levelheaded Cass learn to believe in fairy tales...before her fantasy man disappeared forever?

Don't miss the charming, sexy and utterly mysterious
Michael O'Shea in
ONE UNBELIEVABLE MAN.
Watch for him in February—only from

Silhouette
R O M A N C E™

SPELL2

SPRING fancy '94

They're sexy, single...
and about to get snagged!

Passion is in full bloom as love catches
the fancy of three brash bachelors. You won't
want to miss these stories by three of
Silhouette's hottest authors:

CAIT LONDON
DIXIE BROWNING
PEPPER ADAMS

Spring fever is in the air this March—
and there's no avoiding it!

Only from ▼ *Silhouette*®
™

where passion lives.

SF94

He staked his claim...

HONOR BOUND

by
New York Times
Bestselling Author

Sandra Brown

previously published under the pseudonym Erin St. Claire

As Aislinn Andrews opened her mouth to scream, a hard
hand clamped over her face and she found herself face-
to-face with Lucas Greywolf, a lean, lethal-looking
Navajo and escaped convict who swore he wouldn't hurt
her— *if* she helped him.

Look for HONOR BOUND at your favorite
retail outlet this January.

Only from...

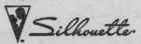

Silhouette

where passion lives. SBHB

Relive the romance...
Harlequin and Silhouette
are proud to present

A program of collections of three complete novels by the most requested authors with the most requested themes. Be sure to look for one volume each month with three complete novels by top name authors.

In January: **WESTERN LOVING**   Susan Fox
                                             JoAnn Ross
                                             Barbara Kaye
Loving a cowboy is easy—taming him isn't!

In February: **LOVER, COME BACK!**   Diana Palmer
                                             Lisa Jackson
                                             Patricia Gardner Evans
It was over so long ago—yet now they're calling, "Lover, Come Back!"

In March: **TEMPERATURE RISING**   JoAnn Ross
                                             Tess Gerritsen
                                             Jacqueline Diamond
Falling in love—just what the doctor ordered!

Available at your favorite retail outlet.

REQ-G3

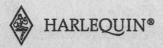   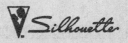

SILHOUETTE... Where Passion Lives

Don't miss these Silhouette favorites by some of our most distinguished authors! And now you can receive a discount by ordering two or more titles!

SD	#05772	FOUND FATHER by Justine Davis	$2.89	☐
SD	#05783	DEVIL OR ANGEL by Audra Adams	$2.89	☐
SD	#05786	QUICKSAND by Jennifer Greene	$2.89	☐
SD	#05796	CAMERON by Beverly Barton	$2.99	☐
IM	#07481	FIREBRAND by Paula Detmer Riggs	$3.39	☐
IM	#07502	CLOUD MAN by Barbara Faith	$3.50	☐
IM	#07505	HELL ON WHEELS by Naomi Horton	$3.50	☐
IM	#07512	SWEET ANNIE'S PASS by Marilyn Pappano	$3.50	☐
SE	#09791	THE CAT THAT LIVED ON PARK AVENUE by Tracy Sinclair	$3.39	☐
SE	#09793	FULL OF GRACE by Ginna Ferris	$3.39	☐
SE	#09822	WHEN SOMEBODY WANTS by Trisha Alexander	$3.50	☐
SE	#09841	ON HER OWN by Pat Warren	$3.50	☐
SR	#08866	PALACE CITY PRINCE by Arlene James	$2.69	☐
SR	#08916	UNCLE DADDY by Kasey Michaels	$2.69	☐
SR	#08948	MORE THAN YOU KNOW by Phyllis Halldorson	$2.75	☐
SR	#08954	HERO IN DISGUISE by Stella Bagwell	$2.75	☐
SS	#27006	NIGHT MIST by Helen R. Myers	$3.50	☐
SS	#27010	IMMINENT THUNDER by Rachel Lee	$3.50	☐
SS	#27015	FOOTSTEPS IN THE NIGHT by Lee Karr	$3.50	☐
SS	#27020	DREAM A DEADLY DREAM by Allie Harrison	$3.50	☐

(limited quantities available on certain titles)

	AMOUNT	$
DEDUCT:	**10% DISCOUNT FOR 2+ BOOKS**	$
	POSTAGE & HANDLING	$_____
	($1.00 for one book, 50¢ for each additional)	
	APPLICABLE TAXES*	$_____
	TOTAL PAYABLE	$_____
	(check or money order—please do not send cash)	

To order, complete this form and send it, along with a check or money order for the total above, payable to Silhouette Books, to: **In the U.S.**: 3010 Walden Avenue, P.O. Box 9077, Buffalo, NY 14269-9077; **In Canada**: P.O. Box 636, Fort Erie, Ontario, L2A 5X3.

Name: _____

Address: _____ City: _____

State/Prov.: _____ Zip/Postal Code: _____

*New York residents remit applicable sales taxes.
Canadian residents remit applicable GST and provincial taxes.   SBACK-JM

Silhouette®